PRAISE FOR DARRELL PITT

'I found myself laughing out loud which rarely happens.'
Sondra Kerby

'An amazing book that has all the elements
of a great whodunnit.'
Ursula Sorensen

'I'm very much looking forward to reading the next book in
the series.'
Alice Hazelbaker

'This was a fun book to read. It had me laughing
a lot throughout.'
Sandy Mill

' I look forward to future installments.'
Caley Gredig

'What an awesome book!'
Michelle

BY DARRELL PITT

The Boy from Earth
Balloon Girls
A Toaster on Mars

Teen Superheroes
Book I: Diary of a Teenage Superhero
Book II: The Doomsday Device
Book III: The Battle for Earth
Book IV: The Twisted Future
Book V: Terminal Fear
Book VI: The Invisible Weapon
Book VII: The Alpha Project

Teen Superhero Bounty Hunters
Book I: Snakebite
Book II: Fear Fight
Book III: Stormfront
Book IV: Past Shadows
Book V: One Small Step

DARRELL PITT

Pizza, Pugs and Murder

A ROSIE RYAN COZY MYSTERY

BOOK FIVE

KENT STREET PRESS

kentstreetpress.com

This edition published by Kent Street Press, 2025

ISBN: 978-1-923360-43-3 (paperback)

ISBN: 978-1-923360-34-1 (ebook)

A catalogue record of this book is available from the National Library of Australia.

For Cleo

1

'Surely there's a law against having ice cream for breakfast,' Kim Chen said.

'If there is,' I said, 'I don't want to know about it.' We were wandering through the monthly Cape Carson Market as we devoured cones of Eddy McCarrick's Homemade Ice Cream. The ice cream maker was famous for having the most flavoursome ice cream on the entire south coast. He only sold it once a month at the town's foreshore market—and it was worth waiting for. 'As far as I'm concerned, dessert should come before dinner. Just in case.'

'You might have something there. Couldn't be anything worse than dying of a heart attack after eating your vegies and leaving behind a full bowl of ice cream.'

I cast my gaze across the market. Almost two hundred stall-holders came together on the first Saturday of each month, selling everything from farm produce to arts and crafts.

I attended whenever I could, usually with an eye on finding

news stories for the Gazette, but there were other benefits to turning up too.

On one side of the foreshore lay our beautiful seaside town of Cape Carson. On the other was the beach and the glistening sea beyond. Today, the air was still and the water flat. Despite being early winter, the sky was a solid sheet of cyan blue, broken only by a flurry of seagulls that chased a fishing boat rounding the breakwater into the bay.

A blob of ice cream dripped onto the grass, and Trixie, my beagle, barked and eagerly licked it up. Today I'd bought double cherry, but she never minded what flavour I purchased. All ice cream was good ice cream as far as she was concerned.

The Cape Carson Brass Band had turned up. Their music played in the distance. I knew a lot of the people in the crowd by sight, but plenty were strangers. Visitors came from across the south coast, many making the most of the weather while they could. Winter on this section of the Australian coastline could be brutal. The clearest morning could turn bad with grey clouds rushing in from the west, forcing visitors to disappear and stallholders to pack up and dash for their cars.

After finishing our ice creams, we stopped at a stall dealing in jams and relish. Both Kim and I were suckers for this stuff.

'You can't beat homemade,' she said, handing over her hard-earned cash for a jar of spicy relish.

'Nothing's better than strawberry jam,' I agreed.

'Isn't that your third jar today?'

'Who's counting?'

'Hello, strangers!'

The voice that came from behind us belonged to my Nan, with whom I shared a house. Eighty-three years old, but with the heart and soul of someone half her age, she was walking hand in hand with her boyfriend, Dave. They had given me a lift to the foreshore in Dave's hotted-up Valiant.

I smiled. It was a pleasure seeing her loving life with a nice guy. The bright light within her had dimmed after the death of my grandfather. Since meeting Dave through a dating website, that light had brightened again.

'Hey you,' I said affectionately and glanced down at the bag in Dave's other hand. 'You've been shopping?'

'A side mirror for a '71 VH Valiant Charger.'

'You needed another one of those?'

He looked sheepish. 'A man can never have too many spares.'

'Or too much useless junk in his garage,' Nan added.

'That too,' Dave admitted.

'Talking about junk,' Nan continued to me, 'you haven't forgotten about the Hospital Trash and Treasure fete?'

I resisted a good old-fashioned eye roll. Forget about it? How could I? Nan had been reminding me about it incessantly for weeks. The Hospital Auxiliary ran the annual fete to raise funds to purchase equipment for the hospital.

People contacted the auxiliary to donate their unwanted goods. While it was a good idea—in theory—it wasn't without its challenges. The fete was held at the Cape Carson Sports Centre. Those who couldn't drop off their goods could arrange pickup by a local volunteer.

That's where my reasonably reliable 2005 Jeep Wrangler Unlimited Rubicon came in handy. The rear seat folded forward, providing space to transport things. Since moving to Cape Carson, I'd been roped into carrying everything from wardrobes to kitchen sinks. One time, I'd even picked up an eight-piece garden setting.

'I'd forgotten all about it,' I told Nan innocently. 'I have no idea what you're talking about. Kim?'

'I've never heard of it,' Kim said, stifling a grin. 'It's news to me.'

'Good,' Nan said, deciding to ignore us. 'I've started getting calls, so I'll be relying on you girls to help out.'

'We can't pick up anything heavy,' I told Nan.

'I'm sure your boyfriend will help out.'

I groaned. 'Todd Parker is not my boyfriend,' I said. Sergeant Todd Parker was in charge at the local police station. 'He's just a friend.'

'So you say. I'm still betting on a wedding before Christmas.'

Nan and Dave gave us a *cheerio* and continued on. Kim,

Trixie, and I angled off down an aisle that specialised in hand-made furniture. These were impressive, but what really got my attention was a nearby stall where the man had bowls carved from various trees: pine, cypress, and olive.

'I've got to have one of these,' I said, picking up an irregularly-shaped bowl made from olive wood.

'What will you use it for?' Kim asked.

'No idea, but you can never have too many dust collectors.' I examined it more closely. 'And this one is lovely.'

After adding the acquisition to my growing hoard, we continued on. My eyes angled up toward Cut Rock Lookout. I'd already been there once today. While taking Trixie for an early morning walk, I'd been hoping to bump into Todd. While we weren't dating, he was one of those guys that was hard to forget. No relationship had eventuated between Todd and me, and it was unlikely that one ever would. Working as a journalist and him as a cop, we were often on opposite sides of the fence.

'So, how *is* it going with Todd?' Kim asked.

I stared at her in amazement. 'Are you reading my mind?'

'Elementary, my dear Rosie. You were gazing longingly at Cut Rock, where I know that you've bumped into Todd more than once. Every time you talk—or think—about him, you get a strange doe-eyed expression.'

'I do not!'

'You do.' Kim glanced past me. 'Plus, you're wearing one of

your favourite dresses.'

It was true. I'd purchased this Zara dress the last time I was in Melbourne. Kim, by comparison, had dressed down for the day, wearing a t-shirt and pair of shorts. The front of the t-shirt had a picture of the writer Truman Capote and a quote: *All writing, all art, is an act of faith.*

I grumbled. 'Nothing wrong with looking pretty,' I said. 'Anyway, I'm busy with work, and Todd seems taken with his friend, Yvonne.'

The attractive brunette had been staying with Todd for the last few weeks. Todd said she was an old school friend, but my imagination couldn't leave it alone. To make matters worse, she was perfectly nice. We'd probably end up being good friends one day.

'They're just catching up on lost time,' Kim said. She nudged me. 'Ah-ha!' she murmured. 'Looks like that dress wasn't wasted after all.'

Two uniformed officers were making their way through the sea of people. One was the lanky form of Constable Jim Turner, but the other was the man himself. The muscular sergeant grinned and gave me a small wave. Smiling in return, I was suddenly worried that I looked doe-eyed, and I quickly rearranged my expression.

'Everything okay?' Todd asked.

'Of course. Why do you ask?'

'You were looking a bit serious. You haven't stumbled across any dead bodies, have you?'

'Not at all!' I had a bad habit of getting involved in murder cases. To be fair, though, I also did my bit in helping to solve them. I shot Kim a look. Doe-eyed! 'I'm fine,' I said. 'Just dealing with my dorky friend. What brings Cape Carson's finest down here?'

Constable Turner answered. 'We had a report of someone stealing honey from a stall,' he said.

'From Ralph Eaglemont's stall?'

His girlfriend, Ellie Applegate, looked after the IT for our office. The pair lived on a farm outside of town, where they raised bees and sold honey at the monthly market.

'That's the one,' Todd said.

'And the Cape Carson Police Department sent our two best cops?' I said.

'That's pretty much it.'

Kim was more critical. 'I didn't know you guys investigated something as small as shoplifting.'

'When people call, we answer,' Todd said.

'That's a great slogan,' I teased. 'Did you write that yourself?'

'Saw it on a bumper sticker.'

Wishing Todd a good day, Kim and I continued down the aisle between the stalls.

'See,' I said to Kim. 'Not doe-eyed at all.'

'You tried hard, but you still looked doe-*ey*.'

'There's no such word.'

'There is now.'

We wandered on until we reached a brightly coloured tent at the end of the aisle. Above the entrance was a professionally made sign that read *The Storytelling Tent* and another smaller sign that read *Tell us your Tales!*

'What's this?' I asked suspiciously.

Kim spoke coyly. 'We're trialling an initiative where local townspeople can get up and tell stories about their lives in Cape Carson. When it's up and running properly, we'll be recording the sessions so they can be saved in the town's historical archive.'

'What a great idea,' I said, then thought a little harder. Kim was the head librarian at the Cape Carson library, with her specialty being local history. 'Hang on. Were you the brains behind this?'

She shrugged. 'Maybe.'

Now that I thought about it, Kim had mentioned this ages ago. I had no idea the whole thing had come to fruition. I felt like a bad friend. 'How could I not know this was happening?' I complained. 'Have I really been that busy?'

'You're always busy. When you're not working, you're busy solving murders.'

'That's just a hobby.'

'Really? Then you should consider stamp collecting; it's safer.'

'So who's running it today?'

'Mina Kabiri.'

I knew her. The slim Persian woman was in her mid-thirties and had an engaging smile. She was the ideal choice to run something like this. We entered the tent, leaving behind the clatter and hum of the market. There were about thirty people scattered about the hundred seats inside the big tent. At the front was a woman I recognised as Marlene Hogan. A Cape Carson Mystery Book Club member, the big, jolly woman owned the local sweet shop on Percy Street.

'...Sam Heath had the shop before me,' she was saying. 'When he retired, I purchased the business, and I've been running it ever since. We still make our own sweets and chocolates and have even moved into liquorice.'

Kim and I grabbed seats at the front. I took out my writing pad and made some notes. This would be a good story for the Gazette. I glanced around and saw one or two familiar faces. Tony Farrell from the local dive business was there. So was my hairdresser, Judy.

Marlene reached the end of her story and sat down as Mina took to the stage. She smiled brightly, displaying a set of sparkling white teeth. 'That was wonderful, Marlene,' she said. 'It's so interesting to hear the history of a local business. Especially all the trials and tribulations you've suffered.'

'And temptations,' Marlene called.

The audience let out a titter of laughter.

'We all give into those sometimes,' Mina said, smiling as she glanced around the room. 'Does anyone else have a story they'd like to share? Something about their life here in Cape Carson? Or a special experience?'

People glanced about, but no one raised a hand.

'Don't be shy,' Mina urged.

Kim leaned close. 'Rosie,' she whispered. 'Get up and tell a story.'

'I'm a journalist,' I murmured. 'I can't report on an event that I'm part of.'

'Anyone?' Mina asked again. 'Does someone have a story to share?'

It seemed for a long moment that no one would speak. Then a tremulous voice came from the back of the room.

'A story?' the voice said. 'I have a story.'

An elderly woman shuffled down the aisle and onto the stage. Lean with porcelain white hair, she wore a flowery dress and an apron decorated with a tiny sunflower print.

Her watery blue eyes gazed out at the audience. She seemed to see people and simultaneously not see them, as if she were blind.

'Hello,' Mina said, smiling. 'Can you tell us your name?'

The woman hesitated as if the question surprised her. 'Celia,' she said. 'Celia Spalt.'

'And what story would you like to tell us?'

'Story?'

The woman looked confused, as if she didn't know where she was.

'Madam,' Mina said kindly. 'We're inviting people to get up and share their stories with us. Is there something you'd like to tell us? You must have seen a lot in your life.'

Celia looked at her in confusion. Then the old lady's eyes focused on me and then Kim. Staring at my friend, her blue eyes shone. 'There's a lot of things I've seen,' Celia said. 'There was that one I saw. The man was minding his own business when it happened.'

Mina exchanged glances with Kim. I could almost read her mind. *This old lady is not well. The poor thing doesn't know what's going on.* Mina looked ready to gently lead the woman from the stage.

'I saw a murder,' Celia said.

This earnest statement was met with voluminous silence. It was almost as if time had stopped. Even the sounds of the market—the voices and the distant music of the local brass band—seemed to fall away. 'The man was murdered. He was minding his own business, and then—*bam*! The other did it.

The other one. Then he was on the ground. I saw it, and I told the one in my house. I told her.'

I stared at the old lady. It was like watching a car crash in slow motion.

Celia nodded earnestly. 'The other one—the one I've known for a long time—she took no notice. I couldn't see more. The trees were in my way. I went out to help. It was easy to get past the one in the house. She talks on that thing all the time. You know the thing?' She turned to Mina, who looked torn between leading the woman off the stage and allowing her to continue. 'So I went out, and the murdered one was in the water. Dead, I tell you. Dead! And I saw the one who did it!'

The assembled audience stared back in silence. I tried to understand what the woman was saying, but it was like trying to decipher an anagram. All the letters were there but in the wrong order.

'I see,' Mina said, although she was obviously clueless. 'Maybe you could write all this down, and then we can get a clearer idea—'

'Celia!' An elderly woman came hurrying down the centre aisle. She was of a thicker build, with her blue-rinse hair in a perm. 'Celia! Where have you been? I've been worried!'

'I told them,' Celia said. 'The man I saw. You know the one. He was in the place...with the water.'

'Yes, Celia,' the woman said, giving an apologetic glance to the audience. 'I'm so sorry. Celia's so quick sometimes. I turn my back for a moment, and she's dashed off somewhere.'

She led the scatterbrained woman back up the aisle and out of the tent. A few audience members murmured to each other as Mina apologised, and asked if anyone else had a story to share.

Kim leaned over. 'What on Earth was all that about?'

'Beats me.'

It was an oddity, a strange event that would have meant nothing, and I would have forgotten.

Except for what happened later.

2

'Welcome!' Giuseppe Costa said, spreading his arms wide. 'Welcome to the new Palladium!'

I wasn't so sure about the word *new*. Leaving Trixie in my jeep, I got out and stared up at the building. It looked like the old cinema hadn't changed at all: it was just as vacant, dusty, and rundown as it had been for the last four years. The vast awning overhanging the footpath—the marquee—was empty of lettering, and the poster frames were blank. As far as I could see, the only difference was the timber bifold doors at the front. These were clean, and the old paint stripped back to reveal the original wood.

It was Monday, and two days had passed since the foreshore market. There were ways I liked to start my week, and they didn't include interviewing Giuseppe Costa. Maybe in his mind, he was a great man in our little town, but to me Giuseppe would always be a corrupt businessman. A small, chubby man with a bad combover, it was hard to believe he was one of the wealthiest property developers on the south coast.

'It's looking very...grand,' I said, struggling for words. 'A beautiful building.'

Giuseppe strolled down the front steps, thumbing back at the theatre. 'Out here, nothing much has changed,' he said. 'All the action's happening inside.'

I followed him into the foyer. Here, at least, he was right. The place was a hive of activity. The Palladium's style was art deco, but age had made it look old rather than stylish. Now, the original tiles on the floor had been polished, the box office had been renewed and cracked mirrors on the walls replaced. The candy counter looked almost ready to serve popcorn and drinks. I felt excited. And a little nostalgic too. This was where I first met Kim. I'd decided to attend a festival of old Hitchcock films. Although it was possible to watch them on DVD, there was nothing like sitting in a theatre and enjoying them on the big screen. I'd just come out of watching *Rebecca*, nursing a container of popcorn in one hand and a large drink in the other, when a woman sidled up beside me.

She was a trim Asian with short black hair, dark eyes, and a mouth that looked ready to break into a smile at any moment. 'How about that Joan Fontaine?' she said in perfect English. 'Beautiful or what?'

I agreed she was. 'I never guessed the ex-wife was so evil,' I continued. 'The housekeeper revered her.'

'You can never tell. Have you read the novel?'

'Yes. It's a classic. People should read more.'

'Ha!' the woman's mouth curved into a big smile. 'Someone who loves books!'

'Guilty, as charged.'

'I'm Kim,' she said.

'Rosie.'

I tried jamming my popcorn under one arm while swapping my drink to the other so I could shake hands, but the lid flipped off my drink, and Coke exploded all over me.

'Oh my goodness!' Kim cried.

I wiped liquid from my chin. 'Don't worry,' I said. 'You'll get used to it.'

We went to the movies a lot after that, but it wasn't to last. Like all cinemas, The Palladium had suffered from a lack of attendance because of competition from streaming services, social media, and a million other digital distractions. Something had to give, and in the end it was the Palladium.

I followed Giuseppe through to the auditorium. This was where the most significant renovations had taken place. The first half a dozen rows of the old cinema had been removed, and a stage erected: live performances would be part of the Palladium's future. The air smelt of freshly cut timber, paint, and cloth. The side walls of the cinema had been repainted Oxford blue with art deco motifs highlighted in white and burnt orange.

Despite never having been a fan of Giuseppe Costa, I had to hand it to him. The place looked stylish, and the Palladium might enjoy a whole new life thanks to him.

Giuseppe took me around the rest of the theatre, and I made notes and snapped a few pictures. The cinema projector was brand new. So was the sound system. No doubt about it, this would be the best cinema for a hundred kilometres. It would bring people to Cape Carson, both for the movies and the live performances.

The businessman had obviously spent a lot of money getting the place back up to scratch. Most of the work had been completed on the interior. All it would take now was a spruce up of the outside, and the theatre would be ready.

'When are you reopening?' I asked as we returned to the street.

'Start of spring,' he said. 'I wanted us ready before then, but that'll give us time to put in all the finishing touches.'

Thanking him, I got into my old jeep, Trixie settled into the passenger seat, and we drove up Percy Street toward the Gazette. I hadn't gone far before I spotted a familiar face at the side of the road and pulled over. 'Hey Nan,' I said. 'Breaking the law again?'

Nan and a group of people had half-covered a street bench in knitted yarn. As members of the newly formed Cape Carson

Yarn Bombers Association, their mission in life was to wrap trees and public items in brightly coloured lengths of knitted or crocheted fabric. I recognised a few members of her gang: Irene Everson, whose husband ran the local pantry shop, and Thelma Rickard, the president of the Rotary club.

Nan's face broke into a cheeky grin. 'The police have driven past a few times,' she admitted. 'It's only a matter of time.'

'We hide around the corner,' Thelma added.

'So you know that yarn bombing is technically illegal?' I said.

'Only if we get caught.'

I wasn't sure that was how the law worked. Trixie and I climbed out, and my beagle immediately allowed herself to be patted by Thelma. 'And isn't yarn bombing usually done under the cover of darkness?' I asked.

'Some of us have poor eyesight,' Thelma said. 'Going out at night is *not* an option.'

'Besides,' Irene added, 'we're doing it for charity.'

'Really?' I asked.

'Shop owners pay us to yarn bomb the street outside their premises,' Thelma explained. 'People hang around to take a look—'

'Which means they're more inclined to also go into the shop,' Nan continued, 'and the money the shop pays us—'

'Goes to Rotary,' Irene concluded.

What a great idea, I thought. *A win-win.*

Still...

'Anyway,' Thelma said. 'The police are good guys—and handsome. Have you seen that new sergeant?'

'Todd Parker?' Nan piped up. 'That's Rosie's boyfriend.'

'He's not my boyfriend—'

'They're out together all the time. Be nice to have a cop in the family. We can all go for rides in his police car—'

I was determined to put a stop to this. 'Todd and I aren't dating, let alone getting hitched, and nobody's going for a ride in a police car.' I nodded to the crocheted fabric covering the seat. 'Unless you ladies get arrested, which I hope doesn't happen.'

Regardless of the outcome, I knew a story when I saw one. Asking the ladies a few more questions, I scribbled notes while I snapped pictures.

'Oh,' Thelma said, just as I put away my notebook. 'And don't forget about the pickups.'

'Pickups?'

Nan intervened. 'I told Thelma you'd offered to pick up donations for trash and treasure.'

Offered? That wasn't my memory of it. I'd been cajoled into it. I shot a look at Nan, who was smiling sweetly. I knew that look. It was horribly similar to a cat with a mouthful of canary!

'Oh...right,' I said. 'Yes. Happy to help out.'

'Great,' Thelma said. 'Nan's got a list of people.'

'Wonderful.' I tried to sound enthusiastic, but there was a slightly more pressing matter I wanted to discuss with Nan. I took her to one side. 'Nan, are you sure you're not overstretching yourself?'

'I do yoga most mornings. I suppose overstretching is the point of it.'

'I don't mean your yoga. I mean, you're involved in every single thing going. The Rotary Club, Lions Club, Hospital Auxiliary—'

'Rosie,' Nan sighed. 'It's better to wear away than rust away. If I can contribute, I will. Besides,' she continued, grinning, 'I don't have to do the heavy lifting.'

Before I could complain about that, she turned away and rejoined her yarnbombing buddies. I thanked them and got back into my car with Trixie, and we continued on to the Gazette. Nan worried me sometimes. She was eighty-three but still carrying on like she was...well, seventy-three. Or maybe even sixty-three. I wasn't sure how eighty-three-year-olds were supposed to behave, but I was sure Nan was nothing like them.

Heading into the Gazette building, I said a quick hello to Doris at reception and our editor, Harry, before heading to the back office. I shared this with Jay Patel, who was currently frowning at his computer.

'Rosie!' he said, pushing back his black-rimmed glasses. 'Thank goodness you're here.'

'What's the emergency?'

'My computer's telling me that I can't say the footy game on Saturday had a climatic ending.'

'That's hardly surprising. Unless a raincloud kicked the winning goal, I think you mean climactic. *Climatic* refers to the climate.'

He sighed. 'What would I do without you?'

'What people did in the old days,' I said, sitting at my desk and nodding to a pile of dusty volumes. 'Dictionaries.'

I transcribed the notes I'd made while speaking to Giuseppe and Thelma. Within half an hour, I had drafts of two articles. Feeling pleased, I sat back and added the files to our shared drive. This way, Harry could take a look at them while I worked on something else.

He sent me a short message:

Great articles. Have you got anything about the Storytelling Tent? Or the Trash and Treasure fete?

Groaning, I quickly replied:

You don't want much, do you?

He wrote back:

It's not easy being the star reporter for the Cape Carson Gazette.

Harry was always especially nice when he wanted something. He sent another message telling me he needed around five hundred words and pictures if I had some. Grumbling, I put a draft together and checked the photos I'd taken at the event. Although the Storytelling Tent hadn't been a fizzer, it hadn't set the town on fire either. I headed up the article, *Locals Share Their Stories,* and sent it to Harry.

Next, I wrote a small piece about the Trash and Treasure fete. There wasn't a lot to say about it yet. Our focus each year was usually on the fundraising side of things or an unusual item that someone had donated.

As not much had been gathered yet, I used photos from previous years to bulk it up.

I spent the rest of the afternoon tidying up some other pieces I'd written over the last few weeks. As well as working on a retrospective of the town's history, I had a few filler pieces, including another story about a proposed Rock and Roll Festival for the town. Sandy Clementine from the diner had been trying to get the project off the ground for some time. The council had just approved a funding grant, so the festival looked to be a goer.

As five o'clock rolled on, I finally called it a day. Not only had I been working almost continuously, but I'd only had one jumbo-sized caramel latte for the day. My average was two, and challenging days had been known to require three.

Grabbing my bag, I had just reached reception when Doris

Glow stopped me. Our marvellous receptionist was peering intently at her computer screen.

'Rosie, did you take these pictures at the Storytelling Tent?'

'Sure. I went with Kim.'

'And this lady got up to speak?'

Rounding her desk, I saw Doris had brought up my article about the event. She was pointing at Celia Spalt. 'Oh, yes,' I said. 'I remember her. She was very confused, poor thing. Dementia, I think. Why do you ask?'

'I reside in the same gated community as Celia,' Doris said. 'She lives there with her friend Violet Smith—or she did. I just had a call from Violet. Celia's dead.'

3

'Dead?' I said. 'What happened?'

'I don't know the full details. It sounds like Celia had a fall in her home. It happened yesterday.'

Disquiet churned in my gut. 'I'm sorry to hear that,' I said. 'How old was she?'

'Seventy-three. But these days, that's not old.'

'Were you friends?'

Doris regarded me sadly with her grey eyes. 'Friends and neighbours,' she said. 'They live next door. Celia's been unwell for some time.'

'Was it dementia?'

'Dementia—and a stroke a few years back. It didn't affect Celia physically, but it muddled her thinking. She found it hard to find the right words. It was frustrating for her. Celia had worked as an editor for one of the big publishers and had loved language. After the stroke, she was forced to speak around the word to explain herself.'

That gelled with how she'd been at the Storytelling tent.

'We can print that photo,' I said thoughtfully. 'You might like a copy. Or her family?'

Doris thought. 'I suppose Violet was Celia's closest family,' she said. 'They were friends for decades. Celia's relationship with her two sons was a little complicated. However, the last photo of their mother might mean a lot to them.'

After promising to arrange copies, I headed out to the car with Trixie. A few minutes later, I arrived home to find Nan on the lounge, busily crocheting.

'Getting ready for another bombing spree?' I asked.

'You betcha,' Nan said. 'This town won't know what hit it.'

I cooked dinner while Nan continued working on her next act of textile terrorism. Despite my cooking not being the same standard as Nan's, I still had a few surprises up my sleeve.

There was a beef stew with dumplings that I'd recently mastered, and I had this ready by the time Nan had completed two more crocheted squares.

While we were eating, I mentioned Celia.

'Celia Spalt's dead?' Nan said. 'I knew her well. Celia used to come into the post office all the time. She and her husband owned a building company. They were pretty hardnosed when it came to business.'

I told Nan what Celia had said in the Storytelling Tent.

'That's pretty strange,' Nan said thoughtfully.

'Seems her mind was on the way out.'

'Really? Maybe you should check. It could be foul play.'

'But if she had dementia—' The look on Nan's face stopped me. 'What?'

Nan clunked down her knife and fork and glared at me with an expression that left me in no doubt as to how she felt. Although Nan was the most loving person on earth, her fiery temper could boil water. 'Rosie Ryan,' she said. 'Maybe Celia had dementia and imagined the whole thing. But you don't know for sure, and that's where the danger lies. She could have been telling the truth and not been able to communicate it.'

'That's possible,' I admitted.

'Just because an old person's mind doesn't work properly, it doesn't mean we ignore everything they say. Old people still need to be treated with *respect*. As if they're *human*. As if they *matter*.' Nan firmly wiped her chin. 'Maybe Celia didn't see a murder. Or maybe she did. The truth is that we don't know.'

Her words echoed in my mind.

The truth is that we don't know.

I felt myself turning red. 'You're right, Nan,' I said. 'One hundred percent.'

'I'm your Nan. I'm always right. Now hand over some more beef stew. I'd hate to see it go to waste.'

After dinner, I rang Doris at home.

'Exactly how unwell was Celia?' I asked.

'Physically, she was pretty good,' Doris said. 'Celia went out every day with Violet. Sometimes to the shops, but at least around the park on our estate.'

'What estate is this?'

'Sandcastle Village. A gated community on Sundial Drive. A wall surrounds the whole estate. There's a park in the middle. If Celia went for a wander—and she sometimes did—then she was fairly safe within the confines of the village.'

'I'm wondering about her mental state. Could she have made things up? Or imagined things?'

'I'm not sure,' she said. 'I don't think so. I never heard her say anything about aliens or goblins if that's what you mean.'

'It is.'

'Celia's problem was finding the right words. That stroke took away her ability to communicate. And she was confused. Sometimes she forgot where she was or what she was doing. At her age and in that condition, things don't get better. They get progressively worse.'

'I see.'

There was a moment of hesitation. 'What's all this about?' Doris asked.

Doris was switched on. Although I didn't know what she'd done before moving to Cape Carson, I'd always suspected there was more to her than met the eye. She'd mentioned working for Foreign Affairs in Canberra, and I knew they were a bright bunch.

'Just a story I'm thinking of doing.'

'Hmm.'

She obviously wanted to probe further but resisted. Thanking Doris, I hung up and got ready for bed. Trixie settled down on the floor beside me. I turned out the light and lay in the darkness.

I saw a murder.

That's what Celia had said. Could there be some truth in that? Could she have seen someone die, and people simply ignored her because she was old? And then the murderer killed Celia to keep her quiet?

The following day, I turned up at work early to talk further with Doris. She wasn't there yet, but Harry was in his office. He was usually the first person in and the last to leave. He glanced up from his desk.

'What are you doing here?' he asked. 'Couldn't sleep?'

I told him about the Storytelling Tent and Celia's death. He nodded thoughtfully when I finished. 'There could be something in it,' Harry said. 'Or the old dear could have been a bit batty.' He shuddered. 'I've always had a phobia about old ladies.'

'Really?'

Harry grimaced. 'I had three aunts when I was a kid,' he confided. 'One was always trying to pinch my cheeks. Another was sure that cabbage soup was the tonic for all of life's problems—and fed me as much of it as possible. The third had a habit of relating the latest adventures of her caged canary, Pablo.' He sighed. 'Believe me, Pablo did not have a thrilling life.'

The front door of the office opened, and Doris hustled in. 'The weather's starting to turn out there,' she said, spotting Harry and myself. 'Hello, Rosie. You're in early.'

'Rosie wants to tap your brain,' Harry said.

I told Doris what Celia had said in the Storytelling Tent. Listening until I finished, she slowly nodded. 'It's hard to say if Celia was confused or really onto something,' she said. 'Her faculties were in a bad way. Having said that...'

She stopped.

'What is it?' I asked.

'We did have someone die recently.'

'Really?'

'Joe Porter.'

That name rang a bell. Not a loud bell, but a distant tolling. 'What happened to him?' I asked.

'You remember I mentioned our park? Well,' she amended, 'we call it a park. It's bushland, really. A few acres were left untouched while the estate was built around it. There's a pond in the middle and a few paths. A big storm came through about a month ago. It was very wet, and the paths can be slippery after rain. There are stepping stones that cross the pond. Joe was found face first in the water. It looks like he slipped on one of the stones, hit his head, and drowned.'

'It must have been a bad fall,' I said.

'He hit his temple. Four bones meet at that spot, and there's a major artery beneath it. That's why a hard blow can kill someone.'

I didn't stop to wonder how Doris knew all this. She was somewhat of an enigma herself and I sensed she wanted to stay that way. Harry had been listening from his office. He called out. 'And drownings can happen in only a few inches of water,' he added.

'But that's usually only among small children.' I paused. 'Why didn't the police look into this?'

Doris answered. 'Probably because there'd been a similar accident only a few weeks before. Hannah Foyle, another woman who lives on the estate, slipped on the same stones and sprained her ankle.'

I nodded. 'So it's a gated community,' I said. 'You must all know each other pretty well.'

'We do.'

'Having two deaths in a month must be a shock.'

'I went to see Violet last night,' Doris said. 'She's upset, of course. Violet knew Celia for most of her life. I haven't had a chance to speak to anyone else. I'm sure they're saddened by

Celia's passing.'

There was something she wasn't saying.

'And Joe Porter?' I prompted.

'We weren't so upset when Joe died.'

'Why?'

'He'd argued with everyone on the estate at one time or another.' Doris hesitated. 'And he had a sly manner about him. Nasty things happened. Vandalism and the like. Everyone suspected it was him, but it was never proved.'

'So if anyone deserved to get murdered, it was him?' I said half-jokingly.

'Let's just say that people weren't particularly unhappy to see him go.'

Harry came to the door of his office and leaned out. 'Doris, would you be happy to show Rosie around the village?'

'Sure.'

'Great. Rosie, go take a look. Get the lay of the land and see if there's anything in this.'

Harry had an excellent journalistic instinct and was wise enough to know when something warranted further investigation.

Doris pointed to her desk. 'What about the phones?'

'Ellie and Jay will be in shortly. They can help look after things for a while. Besides,' he added, 'I've been known to answer a phone or two in my time.'

'Just one thing,' I said. 'I'd like to take Kim along as well.'

Harry's face fell. 'Kim?' he said. 'Your friend, Kim?'

'How many Kims do you think I know?'

'Does she have any investigative skills?'

'What?' I stared at him in astonishment. 'Are you kidding? She's my Watson! Or my Holmes! Or...something!'

'And this is the woman who keeps submitting pictures for Nature Corner?'

Half a page of the paper was put aside for nature pictures submitted by locals. 'Yeah,' I said, folding my arms. 'And?'

'They're terrible.'

Just as I was able to angrily retort, I stopped myself. 'Okay,' I admitted. 'Kim's not the greatest photographer, but she has a good mind for this kind of stuff. She's a librarian.'

'All right,' Harry reluctantly agreed. 'Just as long as she doesn't pass herself off as the Gazette's photographer.'

'Oh no,' I said, crossing my fingers. 'Kim won't do that.'

Doris and I picked up our bags and headed outside with Trixie. Doris had been right. The sky was clear, but a cold wind had sprung up. I rang Kim to see if she was available.

'I've put in so many extra hours at work,' Kim said, 'that I've been having trouble sleeping,' she said. 'I've even been counting books in my sleep.'

'Then getting out will do you good.'

Kim paused. 'It's funny, though,' she said. 'I didn't think

Harry liked my photos. He keeps rejecting them from Nature Corner.'

'It's a very competitive part of the paper.'

Telling Kim I'd see her soon, I hung up. Doris left for Sandcastle Village. After picking up Kim, I drove up into the hills to the estate on Sundial Drive. It lay in a shallow treelined basin about a kilometre inland. I could immediately see why it was called a gated estate. A six-foot high brick wall surrounded it. At the front was a pair of double gates that Doris opened via a remote in her car. We drove into after her.

Sandcastle Village looked to be about the same size as a typical city block. The road came around in a big loop with houses around the exterior. In the middle lay the park Doris had mentioned. Her home was at the opposite end from the gates.

There were around a dozen homes, all large and spacious, with a boundary wall running along the back.

This must have been expensive to buy in.

I remembered what Doris had said about the park. She was right. It wasn't so much a park as the last remaining remnant of natural bushland.

'Wow,' Kim said. 'It's a different world in here.'

'People live in these places for the security,' I said. 'The gate and walls give some measure of protection.'

'I've got a cousin who lives in a gated estate—it's called

Barwon Prison.'

I'd never been to Doris' home before.

Although it was similar to the others, she was obviously a keen gardener. Surrounding her house was an English-style cottage garden jammed with azaleas, clematis, and camellias. I remembered that she'd brought fresh roses into the office more than once from her garden.

Kim and I pulled into the driveway after her and climbed out. Trixie immediately went scampering about.

She could obviously see and smell a thousand things that needed investigating. I called her back and slipped her a home-made doggy snack.

'This is lovely,' I said to Doris. 'Very quiet.'

'I wanted a safe location. The older I get, the more concerned I get about my security.' She leaned closer. 'Mind you, it doesn't seem any safer in here than out there. First, there was Joe. Now there's Celia.'

'They could just be coincidences.'

'I hope so.'

We followed Doris into her home. It was as pretty as the outside and neat as a button. The place was more modern than I'd expected, with Australian landscape prints decorating the walls. It all had a very cozy feel to it.

'This is lovely,' Kim said. 'You've got a good eye for design.'

Doris gave us a quick tour of her home, finishing with her

backyard.

Beyond a thick border of bushes was the wall surrounding the estate. She led us back out the front. 'I'll give you the cook's tour of the other houses,' she said. 'My neighbours are quite a bunch.'

'Really?' I said. 'A bunch of what—exactly?'

Doris laughed. 'They're an interesting crowd,' she said. 'Everyone's different.' Doris pointed to the house next door. 'That's where Celia lived. The car's not there, so Violet's gone out.'

'And Violet is Celia's friend?' Kim said. 'We saw her at the Storytelling Tent the other day.'

'They knew each other for years. They were together for so long that there were all kinds of rumours about them being a couple, but that was just talk. It was a good friendship.' We walked past the house. The place was a two-storey Edwardian with rose bushes along the front. We continued past it to a modernistic art deco building made of glass and curved white concrete. Two cars were parked in the driveway: a late model BMW and an older style Ford. 'This place belongs to Naya Kapoor. She's some kind of psychotherapist.'

Naya clearly loved her garden. She'd transformed the front yard into an island paradise with palm trees, rockeries, ponds, and bromeliads.

'Although,' Doris continued, 'Naya has a personal assistant

who seems to do everything. Ramona, her name is. I've even seen her gardening.'

The next house was a flat bed of lawn with an alyssum border. A low-lying white picket fence ran along the front.

'Trudi Kendrix lives there,' Doris said. 'She works in IT. Works from home, I think. Attractive woman. Has a few men friends around.'

That made me wonder about visitors. 'How do people get into the estate?' I asked.

'You can buzz people in via the intercom. It's not a bad system.'

'Not foolproof, though,' I said. 'A determined criminal with a bit of effort can climb over the wall. Or tailgate someone entering.'

'You're right. It's not perfect, although it's better than it looks. Alarm sensors run along the top of the wall. If someone tries to climb over, a silent alarm is sent through to the base. The cops have turned up a few times because kids have tried getting in.'

Not bad, I thought.

We passed the gates facing the road. Again, I had the strange feeling of being locked away from the rest of the world. I wasn't sure if that was a good thing or not.

'That's Luca's place,' Doris said. 'He's our local Spanish gigolo.'

'Really?' Kim said.

'Down girl,' I said.

'What? A girl can hope!'

Doris shook her head wearily. 'He *thinks* of himself as a ladies' man,' she said. 'But Luca's sixty going on forty with more oil in his hair than a Texas oilfield. If he stood too close to a fire, his head would burst into flames.'

Kim shook her head sadly. 'You really know how to sing a man's praises.'

'He can sing his own praises—and will. Luca sees anything in a skirt as fair prey.' Doris shrugged. 'We've learned to deal with him.'

We continued on. The house beside Luca's was a two-storey neo-classical place with columns and big windows. 'The next home on our tour belongs to Hannah Foyle,' Doris said. 'She owns a dog.'

'I can tell.' A constant, frenzied barking was emanating from the home's interior. 'What's she got?'

'A pug, and get used to the barking. It goes on day and night. Fortunately, she's not too close to my place, so I don't notice. But there's been complaints.'

I nodded. The next property belonged to a couple named Henry and Olivia Rudd. Doris explained that he was a retired university professor, whereas Olivia used to be a bookkeeper.

'Henry's the unofficial security guard for the estate,' Doris said. 'I suppose every place has someone like him. He does everything from running the body corporate to picking up pieces of stray rubbish. He also takes everyone's bins out to the street, although we're all supposed to take our own.'

'He sounds quite energetic.'

'It keeps him busy, but I imagine he wants that.'

'Why?'

'His wife, Olivia, is a little odd. Henry's never said a lot about it, but they had a son who was killed in an accident. Apparently, Olivia's never been the same since. She's—how would you say it—off with the pixies? Have you ever known anyone like that?'

I gave Kim a wide-eyed look. 'Never.'

She punched my arm. 'Idiot!'

But she laughed when she said it.

The next house was the biggest of the lot, an antebellum place with an expansive lawn. Although the grass looked like it had once been well kept, it was now overgrown and badly in need of a mow.

'Hello, Tara,' I said.

'That was Joe Porter's place.'

'He's the one who died?' Kim said.

'Yep. I'm pretty much the only person who didn't argue with Joe, and that's because I made a point of avoiding him. I try to live a quiet life. Even poor Violet fought with him. The man said Celia should have been in a madhouse.'

'That's a horrible thing to say!' I said.

Doris nodded. 'No one was unhappy when he died,' she said. 'No one.'

4

'And now we're almost back home,' Doris Glow said. 'My other next-door neighbour is Vincent Orr.' She pointed to a gothic-style home with an upstairs balcony. The front lawn had been ripped out. Rolls of turf lay nearby, waiting to be laid.

'Obviously a keen gardener,' Kim said.

Doris sighed. 'There's a story around that,' she said. 'Something to do with the lawn being poisoned.'

'Really?'

'I try not to pry. It's easy to get drawn into things, and then people want you to take sides.

'What's Vincent like?' I asked.

'Not one of my favourite people. He lives with his son, Graham. And before you ask,' Doris said, lowering her voice, 'Graham is downright strange. He's home-schooled for some reason that I've never understood. Although he's probably better off being kept away from other children.'

'What makes you say that?'

We'd reached Doris's place again. It was nice to see her cheerful front yard packed with flowers and bushes.

Doris continued. 'I saw Graham throwing rocks at a stray cat in his backyard one day,' she said. 'He was terribly cruel. I called out, telling him to stop, and he yelled something rude at me. So, I went to see his father, who told him to behave.' She paused. 'A few days later, I saw the cat dead in the gutter outside my house. Its head was bloody, as if someone had beaten it with a hard object. I looked at the window of Graham's room—it's that one at the front—and he was staring out, laughing at me.' She shivered. 'Horrible little creature.'

The distant metal gates of the estate clanged open, and a car came up the road and pulled into Celia Spalt's driveway. There was no mistaking the woman who got out: Violet Smith. With her blue rinse, she'd stand out in any crowd.

She looked like she'd aged twenty years in a day.

The poor thing, I thought. *She must be distraught.*

'Violet?' Doris called. 'Can we have a word?'

The elderly woman tried smiling, but it came across more like a grimace as we approached. Doris hugged her as tears spilled from Violet's eyes. We introduced ourselves and offered our condolences.

'We saw both you and Celia at the Storytelling Tent on Saturday,' I explained. 'This must be so terrible for you.'

'I've just been with the police,' she said, brushing tears away. 'They're suggesting I was negligent. That I should have been here to look after Celia.' She spread her hands. 'But I couldn't be here twenty-four hours a day! Celia still had a mind of her own. She didn't always want to come out shopping, and I couldn't force her. Sometimes I had to leave her at home.'

Doris motioned to Violet's house. 'Maybe we can step inside,' she said. 'I can make you a tea? Or coffee?'

'It's all right,' Violet said. 'I can make it.'

We trailed inside after her. The house was large but was still somehow cozy.

A cedar staircase in the foyer led to a mezzanine. The interior was crowded with antiques and old furnishings. An oak sideboard and colonial cedar bookcase crowded the dining room. Vintage display cabinets held crockery and figurines. Prints of paintings by McCubbin and Streeton decorated the living room.

This is quite a collection, I thought. *Almost like an antique shop.*

Violet led us through to the kitchen, where she made coffee. She nodded absently to a row of cocker spaniel paintings.

'Celia liked dogs,' Violet said. 'She always owned one. Back in the old days, at least.'

The woman looked tearful again. Trixie whined. She could always tell when someone was upset. Doris took charge of the tea making, and we were soon nursing warm cups around the dining room table. I told Violet that Kim and I would be visiting the estate over the next few days to do a story about living in a gated community.

Violet gave a wan smile. 'You better not tell the truth,' she said. 'It's not all it's cracked up to be.' She glanced at Doris. 'Sorry.'

'No apologies required,' Doris said. 'There's been some ups and downs. Especially of late, what with Joe Porter and now Celia.'

I told Violet that I'd been intrigued by what Celia said at the Storytelling Tent.

'That she'd seen a murder?' Violet sighed. 'She'd mentioned that to me once or twice too.'

'Could there be any truth in it?' Kim asked.

Violet hesitated. 'Celia was quite confused,' she said. 'She suffered a stroke a few years back. It affected her badly. There was some dementia as well. She would lose things. And take things that weren't hers.'

'You mean stealing?' I said.

'What did she take?' Kim asked.

Violet led us into what had once been a sunroom at the front, but had been converted into Celia's bedroom. It was both lovely and sad to look at. The room was lilac with paintings of roses on the walls. An old teddy bear sat on a seat by the bed. A few photos of Celia and her family decorated a dressing table. Celia was beautiful as a young woman, and her husband was also handsome. A big man, stocky and robust. The sons resembled their father.

Opening a drawer, Violet showed us an odd collection of items: a scarf, tennis ball, silver fork, a grey and red rock, jar of honey, and bottle of shampoo. 'She did this all the time,' Violet said. 'Picked up things. Stuffed them in her apron and brought them home. Half the drawers in the house are jammed with odd things.'

'Goodness,' Doris said. 'I had no idea.'

'I didn't like to tell people. Celia didn't even know she was stealing. She just saw things she liked and took them.'

'Talking about seeing things,' I said, wanting to get back to the purpose of our visit, 'Celia mentioned seeing a murder. You said she'd mentioned it before?'

Violet shrugged. 'I honestly don't know what to say,' she said. 'We led quiet lives. Lots of TV. A few walks. When we were younger, we went on overseas holidays. We still would.' The woman stopped, tears brimming her eyes again as she remembered her lost friend. 'It was her illness that stopped us. Anyway, one day we were watching something on TV when she let out a yell and started blabbing. You know how she was. Confused. Couldn't get the words out properly. I thought she was talking about a movie she'd watched.'

'Did she mention anyone's name?' Kim asked.

'No.'

I tried to remember back to what Celia had said at the tent.

The man was murdered. He was minding his own business, and then—bam! The other did it. The other one. Then he was on the ground. I saw it, and I told the one in my house. I told her.

The *other one* did it. That would seem to indicate the killer. The *one in my house* had to be Violet. Yes, almost certainly Violet. What else had Celia said?

I couldn't see more. The trees were in my way. I went out to help. It was easy to get past the one in the house. She talks on that thing all the time. You know the thing?

Yes. I know the thing. It's called a telephone. But I could understand Violet's issue. Poor Celia must have been blabbing at her all day, half of it non-sensical. It would have been almost impossible to decipher reality from fantasy.

I crossed to the window and peered out. From here, you could see most of one side of the road leading to the gates and a good portion of the park. The bush was thick, although a bare patch between two trees allowed an uninterrupted interior view. I saw something dark that could have been a large rock or a path.

'There was a man named Joe Porter who died last month,' I said. 'He drowned?'

'It was a freak accident,' Violet said. 'He drank a lot. Fell, hit his head, and drowned in the pond.' She hesitated. 'You don't think—'

'We don't know what to think,' I said quickly. I didn't want Violet blaming herself for not listening to Celia. Being a carer for a person with dementia was challenging at the best of times. 'Do you recall how long after Joe's death that Celia mentioned the incident?'

She thought. 'A week?' Violet's brow furrowed. 'Maybe two?'

'Violet,' Kim said gently. 'Can you show us where Celia had her accident?'

The woman led us back to the foyer. I peered at the stairs and the mezzanine above. At the bottom of the stairs was a childproof gate, similar to one you'd see at a kindergarten.

'I had this gate installed to stop Celia from going upstairs. It was to keep her safe. Although I didn't think a fall over the balcony was likely, I thought she could trip and fall down the stairs.' Violet demonstrated the gate. 'Celia could never get the latch to release. It's built with a double release. I thought it was safe to leave the house for a while. I'd lock the front and back doors and leave Celia to watch TV while I went out to shop.' Her voice was full of dread. 'This is what doesn't make sense. How did she get through the gate? And how did she get up the stairs? If she really was murdered—'

'Then it wasn't your fault,' I said. 'You couldn't be here all the time. Did Celia have any other carers?'

'Her son, Leon, always came over on Wednesdays to take Celia out for the day. Her other son, Glenn, has had very little to do with Celia over the years. It was me the rest of the time.'

'It must have been very tiring,' Doris said.

'Exhausting,' Kim added.

'I was prepared to do it. Celia and I were best friends for fifty years.' She pointed to the upper landing. 'The police say that Celia fell from the landing. How could that be an accident?'

I thought back to the Storytelling Tent.

I saw a murder.

There were still lots of unanswered questions. 'And what time did you go out?' I asked.

'I left just after lunch,' Violet said. 'That would have been after twelve. Celia and I ate early.'

'Did you always go out at that time?'

Violet nodded. 'Yes,' she said. 'I'm a creature of habit.'

So all the neighbours knew that Celia would be alone, I thought.

'And what time did you return?'

'Sometime after two o'clock. That's when I found her—' Violet stopped as tears threatened again.

'Violet,' I said, gently. 'Let's assume a worst-case scenario. Suppose there was a killer. How would he—or she—get in the house?'

'Celia would have answered if someone knocked at the door. She wouldn't know a friend from a stranger.' Violet paused. 'Even if Celia didn't answer the door, there's a spare key under the flower pot. It's been there for years. Half the neighbourhood could have known about it.'

'Would Celia follow a stranger upstairs?'

'I don't know. She could be terribly trusting. That's why Sandcastle Village worked for us. We were protected from the outside world.'

Doris spoke. 'You mentioned Celia's sons?'

'Leon and Glenn. They barely speak to each other.'

'And Leon's been taking his mum out on Wednesdays?' Kim said.

'Even that wasn't ideal. Leon has a short fuse. He would get frustrated with Celia and lose his temper.'

'Was he ever violent?' I asked.

Violet hesitated. 'No,' she said. 'But once, he got so furious that I asked him to leave. In fact, I practically pushed him out the door.' She stared up the staircase. 'Is this my fault? Maybe I should have seen this coming—'

Tears trickled down her face again, and Doris comforted her. 'There, there,' she soothed. 'You did your best under difficult circumstances.'

I glanced about. The house was probably worth a lot of money. The paintings were prints, but the antiques looked real. I was no expert, but they looked valuable. 'Violet,' I said. 'I'm sorry, but I must ask this: who inherits all this now that Celia is gone?'

Violet wiped away tears. 'Celia's will was made several years ago. A few paintings are being donated to the Cape Carson Art Centre. A cousin in Perth gets a few items. Other than that, I inherit one-third, as do each of her sons.'

I nodded. People had been murdered for less. Much less.

The chances of Violet being the killer were virtually zero. By her own admission, she'd known Celia for fifty years. Why kill her now? Violet wasn't young. If she wanted the money, it would have made sense to kill Celia years ago to give her time to enjoy the proceeds.

Celia's announcement at the Storytelling Tent was a far more likely scenario. The day after announcing that she'd seen a murder, Celia had mysteriously fallen to her death. Her killer must have heard her speaking in the tent.

'Violet,' I said. 'Did you see anyone from the estate at the tent?'

She shook her head. 'I don't know. I went into a panic after I lost Celia. When I finally peered in the tent and saw her speaking, I whisked her away without looking sideways.' Her gaze met mine. 'Did anyone take photos?'

This had already been going through my mind. I'd thought back to the tent and the cursory glance I'd given the crowd.

Although I'd taken a few pictures, most were of the speakers, and only one had been of the crowd. It was a terrible shame, although I hadn't thought the pictures could be clues for a possible murder investigation.

I brought up the single picture I'd taken of the audience on my phone and showed it to Violet and Doris. 'Do you recognise anyone?'

Both women studied the picture, but their answers came back negative. Kim had opened her phone and was examining her photos.

'Kim,' I said. 'How about you?'

'Er...'

'Kim?'

She showed us her pictures. Like me, she'd also taken a few of the speakers, although they were in darkness while the tent beyond was in bright light. There was a decent picture of Mina. The other photos...

'Kim,' I said. 'What are these?'

She reddened. 'The inside of my handbag.'

'Very...abstract.'

'I've really got to work on my photography.'

Violet spoke up. 'Come to think of it, someone did drop by at about eleven on Sunday,' she said. 'Vincent.'

Vincent Orr? I thought. *The man with the strange child?*

'What did he want?' I asked.

'He's an antique dealer,' Violet said. 'It's not the first time he's dropped by. In fact, it's become a regular occurrence. Every few weeks, he'd stop in and ask about buying Celia's antiques.'

'But if they belonged to Celia—' I began.

Violet's face darkened. 'Exactly,' she said. 'It really annoyed me. Although I told him repeatedly that the antiques belonged to her, he kept asking if we could part with a few pieces. He treated Celia as if she didn't exist.'

'Would Celia have wanted to sell anything?' Kim asked.

'Not even when she was well. Buying antiques had been a lifelong passion, and Celia was always interested in owning. Not selling.'

'Would you be able to tell if anything was missing?' I asked, glancing about. 'It's a big house.'

Violet hesitated. 'Not if it were something small. Celia had dozens of small items in display cabinets. Some are valuable. Others she bought simply because she liked them.'

I decided to come clean, and told Violet that I wanted to investigate Celia's death. 'It may have been an accident,' I said. 'It probably was. But if there's a chance that someone killed her—'

'Then we need to know,' Violet said, firmly. 'Of course. Do what you must.'

I told her we'd do it under the guise of writing a lifestyle piece. After thanking Violet, we returned to the footpath at the same time as a man emerged from the park. He gave us a small wave.

'Speak of the devil,' Doris muttered. 'That's Vincent.'

The antique dealer was a big lumbering man, sixtyish with an untidy beard and a tweed suit. 'Doris,' he said. 'You've been visiting the recently bereaved?'

Doris introduced us.

'The recently bereaved?' I asked.

'Oh,' Vincent said, waving a hand. 'That's how I think of Violet. She was with Celia for so long that I always think of them as an old married couple. How is she doing?'

'As well as can be expected,' Doris replied. She explained that she worked with me at the Gazette and that Kim was one of our photographers. His eyes lit up when she said we wanted to do a story on the estate.

'An article about Sandcastle Village?' he said. 'Wonderful. Mind you, we've had a few deaths lately, but don't let that put you off.' He leaned close. 'Although, there could be more to Celia's death than meets the eye.'

We huddled together. 'Really?' I said. 'What do you mean?'

'I caught a glimpse of someone heading in the direction of Celia's place on Sunday. I think it was Leon.'

'Her son?' Doris said.

'I think so. I can't be sure, but it looked like him from a

distance. He was wearing overalls, and Leon owns some kind of panel-beating place.'

'About what time was this?' I asked.

'After midday.'

'Did you tell the police?' Kim asked.

Vincent shrugged. 'I'd rather not get involved,' he said. 'And it looks like the police are happy to accept that Celia fell off her balcony.' A smile split his face. 'Fell off her balcony! Sounds like she fell off her perch! Like a bird!'

Although he roared with laughter, the three of us only smiled politely. Yes, I thought. Ha-ha. A lovely old lady dies tragically, and you're making jokes about her.

'I understand you also visited Celia on Sunday?' I said.

'That was earlier,' he said. 'And purely a business call. Late morning. I deal in antiques, and Violet and Celia have a decent collection of Royal Doulton. I have an interested buyer. Anyway, better get moving. I try to walk ten thousand steps a day, and I'm way behind.' Saying goodbye to us, Vincent arrowed for a path leading into the park and disappeared.

Okay, I thought. *Leon visited Celia—and a third of the estate goes to him. Could Leon have murdered his mother?*

5

I glanced at my watch and told Doris we had to get going. She gave us a remote control for the gates so Kim and I could come and go as we needed over the next few days. We returned to my jeep and drove out.

I immediately felt a sense of relief. 'Do you feel that?' I said to Kim. 'Like we're escaping Alcatraz?'

'You're not wrong there,' she said. 'The whole place has a weird vibe.'

Trixie whined.

'Even Trixie agrees,' I said. 'What did you think of what Violet said?'

'Which part? Celia shouldn't have been able to get to the upper floor, yet she did. If she were murdered, it was probably someone who heard her at the Storytelling Tent. Or one of her sons. It sounds like Leon may have visited the day she died.'

'We'll speak to all the neighbours,' I said. 'But I want to talk to Todd first.'

'Then drop me off at the library. I've got a few things to do.'

I dropped Kim at her work before continuing down to Percy Street. It wasn't far from here to the police station, and both Trixie and I needed a walk. She needed the exercise, and I needed to think. I was passing the bakery when I saw a familiar couple coming towards me.

Oh-oh.

I hightailed it across the road to the coastal path that trailed alongside the beach. All the while, I felt like a coward, but I didn't care. Taking refuge behind a tree, I saw my ex-husband George and his girlfriend, Sadie, go into a shop.

Trixie turned her head quizzically towards me.

'Yeah,' I said. 'I know. I should speak to them, but it's too soon.'

George's brother Nico had recently gotten into serious trouble, and I was the person who'd brought him unstuck. I hadn't done anything wrong, but the brief meetings I'd had with George since had been so icy that a penguin would have caught cold.

Whining, Trixie rubbed her head against my leg. 'It's okay,' I said. 'Healing takes time.'

It was a shame that our lives had been turned upside down. George and I had been getting on okay. I'd even formed a friendly relationship with his new, no-nonsense girlfriend, Sadie.

Trixie and I headed along the path, finally crossing over to get to the police station on First Avenue.

Constable Jim Turner was at the front counter typing when we entered. 'Ah-ha!' he said. 'Just the person I wanted to see.'

'Who? Me?'

'Sure, Rosie. I need some advice. Some *female* advice.'

I frowned, hoping this wasn't to do with his love life. He had enjoyed a not-so-secret crush on a goth girl named Samantha Greco for a long time. With any luck, Jim may have turned his attention to someone else. I thought the chances of a relationship between him and Samantha were somewhere between zero and less than zero. If that were possible.

'Okay,' I said. 'I do have some experience at being female. Quite a lot, really, being one myself.'

'It's about Samantha.'

I groaned internally. 'From the Hot Spot?'

That was the local Cape Carson bakery.

'And our gaming group,' Jim said.

'Oh, that's right,' I said, remembering. 'What's that game you play? A Steam Train in Robotville?'

'A Steamcar in Dinosaur Town,' he admonished me. 'You'd remember if you ever came along to play.'

'I'd love to, but that's when I get my nails done.'

'You don't even know what night we meet.'

'I get my nails done *every* night; I have a lot of nails.'

'Well,' he said, ignoring me. 'I've decided to ask Samantha out.'

'Out? Where?'

'On a date! Where else?'

I tried to imagine them as a couple and realised my imagination had limits. I couldn't see them together. They were nothing alike. He was tall and conservative, and she was short and a goth queen. Samantha was lovely but probably prowled cemeteries at night in a search for undead demons.

Cape Carson had its own witch's coven, which I hadn't visited yet, but intended to. It wouldn't surprise me if Samantha were an active member. Working at the bakery, she probably supplied them with effigies made of human-shaped loaves that they stuck needles in or cast love spells over.

Still, who was I to stand in the way of true love?

'Okay,' I said. 'So what *female* advice are you after?'

'Flowers. I'm thinking of sending her some.'

'All right.'

'And maybe taking her to dinner. Somewhere nice.'

'Right.' I tried to process this. 'Okay. Roses are probably a safe option. Maybe blood red because she probably likes...well, blood. As far as eating goes, if you're after something fun and friendly, then you can't beat Sandy's Diner. If you're after something more upmarket, then Francesca's. People say it's the best Italian restaurant in town.'

Jim looked at me with new respect. 'Rosie,' he said. 'That's great advice. Now let me do a favour for you.'

'Okay,' I said uncertainly.

'Do a story about our board game.'

I tried not to roll my eyes. A lot of people said those words *You've got to do a story about,* and mostly they were subjects about which I shouldn't do a story. Sometimes it was cats. *Do a story about my cat Bill. He died last week, and he's sending me messages from Cat Heaven.* Other times it was hobbies. *Do a story about my collection of belly button fluff. I've been collecting since I was eight.*

One time it was an elbow. A woman rang me saying I should do a story about her left elbow because she could use it to predict the weather. I rarely hang up on people, but her I hung up on.

I was about to make an excuse when I thought about how Harry was always saying the newspaper survived on pictures. He said people loved seeing photos of people they knew, and he was right. *Pictures, pictures, pictures!* That's what Harry always said, and a photo of people grouped around a board game could be interesting.

'All right,' I reluctantly agreed. 'When do you meet?'

6

I made my way out to the back of the police station to Todd Parker's office.

The police sergeant looked up from his computer. 'Rosie Ryan,' he said. 'What a pleasant surprise.'

'You're not being facetious, are you?'

'Not at all.'

I sat down opposite.

It was a shame that nothing had happened between us. Besides being good-looking, well-built, and one of the few men who was my height, he was also a genuinely lovely guy.

My thought strayed back to Yvonne.

'Rosie?' Todd said. 'You're staring at me. Did I forget to shave one side of my face?'

'No, your face is perfect,' I said and immediately thought this sounded like flirting. 'I want to ask you about Joe Porter.'

He frowned. 'Okay,' he said. 'The guy who fell over in the pond and drowned.'

'*Allegedly.*'

'Rosie. Please don't tell me this is another one of those *this seemed like an accident, but it was really murder.*'

'First, let me remind you that I've been right more times than wrong. And second, I don't know what it was. All I know is that an elderly woman claimed to have seen a murder, and now she's suddenly dead.'

'Who's this elderly woman?'

I explained to Todd about Celia, the Storytelling Tent, and her subsequent death.

'We've spoken to Violet,' Todd said. 'But I suppose you already know that.'

'She seemed to think you were blaming her for Celia's death.'

'No. Not blaming her. Simply trying to work out what happened. It looked like Violet left that gate unlocked at the bottom of the stairs, and it resulted in a tragedy.'

'She told us she always locked it.'

'Everyone makes mistakes. And it was wide open when we arrived.'

'And Celia saying she witnessed a murder? What do you make of that?'

'It's a stretch. Although I'm not saying it's impossible, it's more likely Celia Spalt got mixed up after seeing an episode of *Columbo* or *Murder, She Wrote.*'

'Just because she was old—'

'Age has nothing to do with it. Dementia is what we're talking about here. In her fuddled state, she saw something on television that she confused with reality. When she got up at the Storytelling Tent, she suddenly remembered what she'd seen and thought it was real.'

What Todd was saying sounded reasonable. Except for one thing.

'So Celia just happened to die the next day after making this announcement at the Storytelling Tent? Don't you think that's an incredible coincidence?'

'She was an old lady. Old people die.'

'Old people also get murdered. And what about Joe Porter? What about his death?'

'Rosie,' Todd said, patiently. 'The man drank a lot. He slipped on some stepping stones crossing a pond, hit his head, and drowned. Another woman, Hannah Foyle, had an accident at the same spot a few weeks before.' He shuddered. 'She owns a pug.'

I tried not to smile. Although Todd loved dogs—he owned a three-legged greyhound named Rocko—he had an aversion to pugs.

Todd brought up some information on his computer. He peered at it intently. 'Hmm,' he said. 'This is interesting. Joe Porter had form.'

'He was a criminal?'

'Some break and enters. A few armed holdups. Looks like he was robbing people using a replica pistol. It was years back. Twenty years ago.' Todd clasped his hands together. 'Tell you what. I'll make inquiries. Do you know if the session at the Storytelling Tent was being recorded?'

'No, it wasn't.'

'That's a shame. Tell you what, though, I'll look into the other people who live on the estate.'

'And you'll tell me if you find anything?'

'No.'

'*What?*'

'Rosie, I can't share information about innocent people. They deserve their privacy as much as anyone.'

I knew I would get nothing more from Todd. I hated it when he was all Mister Policeman with me, and not Todd, my friend. 'Okay,' I said. 'Great. That may lead to something.'

'And what will you do?'

'Kim and I are returning to Sandcastle Village to interview everyone who lives there.' I got up to leave. 'And we'll examine the spot where Joe Porter died.'

Todd sighed. 'You could leave this up to the professionals,' he said.

'Yeah,' I replied. 'But where would the fun be in that?'

7

'It's a good day for a funeral,' Kim murmured.

'You're not wrong about that,' I replied.

Four days had passed since Celia's death. We were at the Cape Carson Crematorium, where her service was being held. Although the rain had held off until we entered the building, a storm had broken the moment the service had begun. Normally, bright sunlight illuminated the stained glass images of trees and Australian wildflowers. Now, however, rain ran down in long rivulets, blurring the images into patches of dull colour.

Celia's coffin sat at the front, ready to disappear into the floor once the service was done. To its left, a slide show played on a projector as the gentle strains of Louis Armstrong singing *It's a Wonderful World* echoed about the timber-clad interior.

Kim and I sat in the back row with Doris. As funerals went, this was a small affair. Violet was in the front row on one side, standing beside a man who had to be one of Celia's sons. On the opposite side of the aisle sat someone I assumed was the other son.

'That's Leon,' Doris said quietly, indicating the man beside Violet. He had longish brown hair, an earring, and tattoos up and down both arms. 'And Glenn's on the other side.'

His brother, Glenn, looked like him, but his hair was messier, and he was unshaved. He wore a suit two sizes too large.

I felt sorry for Celia.

Both her sons looked rough, and I wondered what had produced such men. It was difficult associating these haggard, grown men with the dainty, elderly lady we'd seen.

Kim leaned close and whispered. 'They both look like they're on parole.'

'Leon runs a panel beater's shop,' Doris said. 'I think he does pretty well out of it.'

'What about Glenn?' I asked.

'You know that salvage yard just outside of Barkly?'

I vaguely recalled driving past it. The property was on the outskirts of the tiny town, although calling it a salvage yard was being polite. A high corrugated iron fence surrounded the place. Inside were piles of second-hand building supplies and furniture that looked like they should have been consigned to the dump.

'That's his business?'

'If you can call it that.' Doris nodded slightly to a couple standing in the row behind him. 'That's Olivia and Henry Rudd.'

I cast my gaze over the pair. Henry Rudd was tall—almost as tall as me—but stooping, with greying hair. He wore a brown, corduroy three-piece suit. Doris had said he was a professor, and I got the impression he still saw himself as such. The woman was shorter and obviously much younger than her husband. Where he was sixtyish, she was only about forty with fizzy, mousy hair and a pudgy body. She glanced around.

Something's wrong with her, I thought. At first, I suspected a brain injury, but then this idea was immediately replaced by *no, she looks vague*, like a young child awoken from a deep sleep.

Doris indicated a blonde woman in a short black dress behind them. 'That's Trudi Kendrix.'

The man in the row behind, I recognised immediately.

Vincent Orr was dressed in virtually the same manner as the previous day: a tweed suit and tie. This time, however, he had his son, Graham, with him. There was no resemblance between the two. The boy looked to be about twelve. He had a pasty white face and jet-black hair combed to one side. He wore jeans and an unironed chequered shirt. Almost as if he could read minds, Graham glanced around, saw me staring, and scowled before turning away.

'What a nasty-looking kid,' Kim muttered. 'Like something

out of a horror film.'

Doris gave a tiny nod to the seats behind Violet and Leon. 'The man is Luca Romero,' she said. He wore a white suit and had slick, dyed black hair and a moustache. I recalled Doris saying he thought of himself as a ladies' man. This impression wasn't lessened by the attention Luca was giving to Trudi's legs.

Doris told us the woman beside Luca was Hannah Foyle. She was an overweight woman, maybe around forty, wearing a polka dot dress. In her arms, she nursed a fawn-coloured pug.

The dog gave a single yap, and she silenced it. Trixie lifted her head and looked up at me. *Good dog.* I stroked her head. Trixie knew when to stay quiet.

This left two people from Sandcastle Village. The first was an Indian woman who was behind Hannah and Luca. She was slim and attractive, probably about thirty, with dark hair and big round earrings. Her dress was red and gold and looked expensive. I thought I'd seen something similar in a recent Myers catalogue.

The other woman was younger. Probably about twenty-five and wore a tiny black dress. Her dark brown hair was short, with golden blonde streaks running through it. Her face was eerily reminiscent of a young Audrey Hepburn.

'The Indian woman is Naya Kapoor,' Doris said. 'Her field is motivational psychology.'

'I'm not sure what that is,' I said.

'Me neither,' Kim admitted.

'I don't think anyone's quite sure,' Doris said. 'She does some kind of counselling online. I looked her up once. She talks about people aligning their energies with the universe.' She nodded to the girl. 'And that's Ramona Coxon. She's Naya's personal assistant, although I'm not sure what that involves. Probably everything.'

The celebrant got up to speak. It was an elderly man whom I'd seen perform several funerals over the years. He talked about Celia, detailing how she'd built up a business with her husband before retiring. Celia's husband had died several years before. After that, Violet had moved in with her, and they'd eventually relocated to Sandcastle Village.

Violet was invited to get up to speak. The elderly woman took the few steps to the podium and gazed across the small crowd. 'I knew Celia for almost fifty years,' Violet said. 'She was a good person. One of the best I've known.'

Glenn snorted.

The woman's eyes flashed angrily at him. For a moment, I thought she was about to snap at the man, but she obviously decided that any disagreement she had with him had to wait. Over the next few minutes, Violet described how she had come to know Celia over the years. Despite there being times when they weren't living near each other, they still stayed in contact.

She finished by speaking about the tragedy that had led to her death.

'I don't understand how Celia got upstairs,' Violet said, her eyes moving from one person to the next. 'I always locked the gate. It's almost as if some unseen hand led her up those steps.'

An unseen hand...

There was no doubt in my mind what she meant. This was a direct challenge to Celia's killer. The old woman's eyes moved from one person to the next. I hoped to see some shift in their body language. Some unconscious *give* that they were guilty. Sadly, I spotted nothing. They all stood, silent and unmoving, under Violet's scrutiny.

A crack of thunder rolled across the sky, and the whole building shook.

Someone in this room killed Celia, I thought. *I'm sure of it.*

I glanced at Kim. Tears were rolling down her cheeks. 'Kim,' I murmured. 'Are you okay?'

'I *always* cry at funerals,' Kim said in a low voice. 'Even when it's people I don't know.' She considered. 'Mind you, funerals aren't all bad. You get to wear nice clothing. Meet lots of new people. Eat and drink at the wake if there's one. I suppose they can be quite fun.'

'Yeah,' I agreed. 'As long as you're not the deceased.'

A lot of other people were crying too. Violet: she'd lost a lifelong friend. Trudi and Hannah were dabbing away tears, and the vague expression on Olivia's face had morphed into something unreadable. Confusion, possibly. The only man openly showing any grief was Luca Romero. The Spaniard's face was wet with tears.

The service ended, and people were invited to place a flower on Celia's coffin. Everyone trailed up to the casket, except for Kim and me. Neither of us felt we'd known Celia well enough to contribute. Both Leon and Glenn tarried at the coffin. As Celia's sons, I suppose they had more history to process than anyone else.

Finally, it was done, and the coffin slid away into the floor as a piece of classical music played. The disappearance of the coffin broke the spell, and people turned to each other and chatted.

Leon leaned over and offered a few words of condolence to Violet. Glenn didn't speak to anyone. He turned and left, shooting a single glance at Kim and me as he went.

Slowly, everyone trailed outside. The rain had stopped, and the sun was valiantly trying to break through the clouds. The narrow roads running through the Cape Carson Cemetery were wet. Water dripped off a nearby stone angel. Rosellas chatted and shrieked in a nearby tree.

The crematorium was situated in the middle of the cemetery. I couldn't help but think about my grandfather, Frank Ryan. Although a plaque on a nearby wall celebrated his life, his ashes had been taken out to sea and gently released into the deep waters of the Southern Ocean.

I turned back to the group. Everyone was standing around chatting as they often did at funerals. I was about to ask Doris if she could introduce us to some residents when Luca Romero arrowed over.

'Ladies,' he said grandly, all trace of his grief gone. 'What an unhappy occasion.' His eyes moved to Kim and me. 'But we have friends of Celia I have not met. How did you lovely ladies know our dear neighbour?'

Doris explained that Kim and I were doing a story about life on a gated estate. The transformation in Luca's attitude was instantaneous as his eyes sparkled. 'A grand idea!' he said. 'People will want to live here, meaning the house prices will rise.' He grinned, showing a row of glistening white teeth. 'Rising prices are always good!'

'It must be sad losing one of your friends,' Kim said.

'Friends?' Luca said.

'Celia.'

'Oh! Yes! Of course. A wonderful lady. I wish she were here. Well,' he amended, 'she is with the Almighty now.'

Doris glanced about. 'It's rare to get everyone together at once.'

'Indeed. When was the last time? It would have been one of the barbeques. Would it not?'

'I suppose so.'

I thanked Luca for his time and asked if we could question him later about living on the estate.

'That would be wonderful,' he said, beaming. 'I can always make time for beautiful women.'

Kim forced a smile. 'Lucky us.'

All the mourners had left the crematorium and were piling into their cars. Among the last were Violet and Leon. I made my way over to them.

'...the estate will be divided according to Celia's will,' Violet said.

'But you'll have to move out of the house,' Leon said. 'We can't sell it with you in it.'

'Having me there won't harm its value.'

'It won't help either.'

It looked like their disagreement was about to escalate into a full-blown argument. Fortunately, Leon looked up at that moment.

'Oh, g'day,' he said.

'I'm Rosie.' I introduced Kim to him, and we passed on our condolences.

'Thanks,' he said. 'It's been a tough time.'

'For everyone,' Violet added, giving me a look.

'We're doing a story about living at Sandcastle Village,' I said. 'Some publicity may do the area some good, especially if you're thinking about selling.'

'We're definitely selling,' Leon said.

Violet shot him another look, but I went on. 'It sounds like quite a community,' I said. 'A safe area to live. Neighbours to visit. Barbeques in the park. Did you ever go to the barbeques?'

He nodded. 'A couple,' he said. 'I went there mainly to help keep mum company. She could be a handful sometimes.'

I had to play this carefully. 'You recall Joe Porter? Someone mentioned that he was hard to get on with.'

'Joe Porter? Yeah, I remember him.' Leon thought for a moment. 'Everyone disliked him.'

'Why?'

'He was a rat. He was always doing underhand things to get at people.' He frowned. 'But I know there was a big argument between him and Hannah.'

'What was the argument about?'

'Her dog. Said it was barking all the time.'

Violet nodded. 'It does bark a lot,' she said. 'Continuously.'

'And Hannah and Joe argued about it?' Kim asked.

Leon shrugged. 'I think Joe argued with just about everyone,' he said. 'Mind you, he never worried me. Got lucky with the lottery and ended up here.'

'The lottery?'

'Yeah. I was talking to Joe about it one day. He was living in Geelong when he bought a lottery ticket and won six million dollars.'

Gosh, I thought. *That's six million reasons to want someone dead.*

8

The next thing Kim and I did was investigate the scene of the murder. Not Celia's murder—if she was murdered at all—but Joe's murder, which I also wasn't sure was even a murder.

Doris returned to the office while we went back to the estate. It was almost midday, and Sandcastle Village seemed strangely deserted. Cars were in some driveways. It looked like the Rudds were at home, as was Trudi Kendrix. Hannah Foyle had arrived just ahead of us. The big woman trundled up the footpath, her pug cradled under one arm, and disappeared inside.

Trixie whined, and I gave her a doggy snack. Again, I had that same strange sensation of isolation. 'Do you feel that?' I asked Kim.

She tilted her head as if listening to the wind. 'You mean that weird, otherworldly sensation?' she said. 'As if a hellhole had opened up? As if all the demons of the underworld—'

'Kim!' I snapped. 'Yes, it's a weird feeling, but do you have to enjoy it so much!'

'You know I love horror!'

'Yes, and I love bacon, but it doesn't mean I want to be a pig! Anyway, let's find this spot where Joe Porter died.'

We followed a narrow trail through the bush. The thick vegetation closed in around us.

Within seconds, we were surrounded on all sides by tea trees, wattles, eucalypts, and callistemon. It would be easy to imagine that we were somewhere miles out in the country and not in the midst of a gated community in a seaside town. The only sign of the outside world was the occasional hum of a car as it sped past on Sundial Drive.

We came around a bend in the trail, and it opened out onto what was obviously the barbeque area.

It was larger than I'd imagined, a roughly circular area with a brick barbeque surrounded by concrete seating.

Trixie sniffed around the barbeque, obviously hoping for some remnants of sausages or steak.

'Sorry,' I told her. 'No scraps today.'

The pond lay nearby. It was tiny, barely twenty feet across. Only a few feet deep with a line of stepping stones arcing across the middle. Bush rocks and reeds decorated the edges.

'An Olympic-sized swimming pool,' Kim said, 'it's not.'

'It's deeper than I expected.'

Kim pointed to the other side. 'The trail continues over

there. It looks like it goes towards Violet's place.'

I nodded, my eyes following the trail until it disappeared into the bush. In the distance lay the window of a house. My heart raced. 'Kim,' I said, pointing. 'That's Celia's bedroom window.'

'Wow,' she said, staring. 'You're right.'

I remembered the dark patch I'd seen as I peered out her window at the park. I'd thought it was a rock or path. Now I realised it was the murky water in the pond.

'Rosie,' Kim said. 'You're thinking what I'm thinking?'

'That Celia was in her bedroom when she looked out and saw the murder?' I said. 'It makes sense. She could see everything that happened. Joe Porter had probably just reached the stepping stones when his killer came up from behind. One good whack across the side of the head, and he fell face-first into the water.'

'Poor Celia. She probably couldn't comprehend or verbalise what she saw.'

'She forgot all about it until something triggered it. Celia tried to communicate what she'd seen. Everyone—including us—dismissed her as an old lady who'd lost her mind.'

'It's a shame she didn't tell us the killer's name.'

'At least we know Joe Porter was murdered. Now we just need to work out who did it.'

Trixie pricked up her ears.

'What is it, girl?' I said.

My answer arrived with the sound of a bark and heavy footsteps. Hannah Foyle's pug came scampering down the path and barked wildly at us as Hannah appeared.

'Quiet, Princess!' Hannah called out. 'Mummy's here. Oh—' The woman caught sight of us. 'We've got visitors.'

I smiled and introduced ourselves. 'What a beautiful dog,' I said. 'What's her name?'

'This is Princess,' Hannah said, picking her up and waving her paw like a doll's arm. She peered at us. 'I saw you at the funeral earlier. Did you know Celia well?'

'I work with Doris,' I explained, saying we were doing a feature story on Sandcastle Village.

'Goodness. It's hard to imagine that there'd be anything interesting to say about us. Nothing ever happens. Except for poor Celia.'

'Were you here the day she died?'

Hannah nodded. 'I'm semi-retired,' she said. 'So I have a lot of time on my hands.'

'You didn't see anyone unusual on the estate that day?'

'Not that I recall.' She thought harder. 'I did see a gardener. I thought that was odd. They're not usually here on Sundays. They come every third Monday.'

'Did you get a good look at them?'

'Not really.'

'Around what time was that?'

'After lunch. I'm not sure.'

Kim spoke up. 'I understand someone else died recently.'

Hannah's face darkened. 'Oh *him*.' She peered into the dark water. 'Joe Porter. A horrible man. Always complaining about Princess.'

'Complaining?' I said.

'He said she was making too much noise. Barking all the time.' As if in response, Princess fired off a flurry of barks. 'Ridiculous.'

'I'm sure.'

Hannah leaned close. 'To be honest,' she said, 'people weren't too unhappy when Joe Porter died. He'd gotten every-one offside. He wasn't one of us.'

One of us?

She must have seen the confused look on my face.

'Everyone here is of a certain standard,' Hannah said. 'I don't want to say class because I don't mean that. But everyone here either worked for their money or was born into it. Not so for Joe Porter. He had that lottery win. *Six million dollars.* Before that, did you know he was a handyman? Did home repairs. Fixed appliances and resold them. Then he won the lottery and went from rags to riches overnight.'

'How did it affect him?' I asked.

'Badly!' Hannah retorted. 'People didn't want to hear about

his wealth. And he was a cantankerous old drunk.'

'I've heard his drinking was a problem. Was he often out of control?'

'Well, I had an uncle who was a falling down drunk and ended up dying in a car accident. Joe wasn't like that. He could hold his liquor. No doubt about that. Even when he hadn't been drinking, you could still smell it on him. But he wasn't the type that you'd find lying in the gutter.'

Kim nodded to the stepping stones. 'Although he did slip when he was crossing the stepping stones.'

'It's because they're dangerous. I sprained my ankle trying to cross them one day. They're especially slippery after rain.' Hannah frowned. 'Frankly, Joe hated everyone, and everyone hated him. Joe was horrible about Princess. Always complaining about her. You know what I found one day on my front lawn? Meatballs.'

'Meatballs?' I repeated, mystified.

'They had a horrible chemical smell about them: poison. And it doesn't take a genius to work out who did it.'

'Joe Porter?'

'Obviously. Who in their right mind would ever harm a dog?'

On that point, at least, I agreed one hundred percent with Hannah Foyle.

Princess squirmed in her arms. Hannah's face brightened.

'That's the signal telling me I've got to get moving,' she said, laughing. 'She's a bossy little girl, this one.'

Trixie barked. I imagine she was disappointed that she'd missed the opportunity to make a new friend. Hannah said we could call on her one day if we had further questions. After she trotted out of sight, I turned to Kim. 'What do you think?'

'I think Joe was an entirely unlikeable person,' she said. 'And an alcoholic. No wonder the cops dismissed his death as an accident.'

'I wonder if Hannah could be responsible.'

Kim frowned. 'It's hard to imagine that big lady hitting him over the head with a rock,' she said. 'And why would she? What was the motive?'

'Dislike?'

'Then you'd have to *really* dislike him.' She paused, thinking. 'Let's not forget that six million dollars. That's a strong motive. Whoever inherits his estate may have wanted him dead.'

'I'll find out who that is.' I glanced at my watch. 'In the meantime, I think we should talk more to Leon about his mum.'

'Vicent said Leon dropped by the day Celia died.'

'So he's a suspect,' I said. 'He had a reason to kill his mother: his inheritance. Although that doesn't explain why he'd kill Joe.'

Kim thought. 'The two could be unrelated,' she said. 'We're only assuming they're connected.'

She had a point. Although Celia could have seen Joe Porter's murder, there was no evidence that her announcement at the Storytelling Tent had anything to do with her death. Leon could have simply killed his mother for the inheritance, and Joe's killer was a different person.

'That's true,' I said. 'Although having two murders by two different killers in such a short time would be an incredible coincidence. Let's check with Leon and see what he has to say.'

We returned to my jeep and drove out of the estate. My phone rang: Nan.

'Hey Nan,' I said.

'Rosie,' she said. 'You haven't rung me back. I sent you a message.'

'What?' I glanced at my phone. 'Sorry. I didn't notice.'

'Are you available to do a pick up for Trash and Treasure?'

'Uh...'

'I'll take that as yes. I've already sent you the address, so I'll let Gladys know you're coming.'

'Uh...'

'Bye!'

9

Ten minutes later, we were pulling into the driveway of Gladys Levenson. Gladys lived on the south side of Cape Carson, only a few streets back from the bay. Her neat bungalow was nestled under the boughs of two great jacaranda trees.

Trixie barked.

'I'm glad you're excited,' I said dismally. I wanted to get on with our investigation. Not lug heaps of boxes down to the Sports Centre.

'It might not take long,' Kim said. 'Nan didn't say in her message what needed picking up?'

'Something about some toys.'

'That shouldn't be too bad.'

A knock on the door produced a flurry of barking inside. The door creaked open, and an old lady appeared. 'Gladys?' I said. 'I'm Rosie Ryan.'

'Oh, Rosie!' the old lady said. 'Thank goodness you're here. You can finally take Oscar away.'

'Oscar?'

'He's taking up far too much room.'

We followed Gladys down the hallway to her living room. It was a lovely space with a lounge suite surrounding a television and a vase of flowers on the coffee table. What wasn't so lovely was the eight-foot-high blue and pink stuffed panda that dominated the room. It was huge, butting up against the ceiling and seeming to fill a quarter of the space. How it had gotten in here was a complete mystery.

Kim began. 'What the—'

'Goodness,' I cut in.

'This is Oscar,' Gladys said, introducing the giant panda as if he were a house guest who had just arrived for the weekend. She added unnecessarily, 'He's rather big.'

'Really?' I said. That was like saying the ocean was wet. 'How did Oscar get here?'

He couldn't be a gift. Oscar's grin quickly dispelled that possibility. It wasn't a friendly grin. Not in the slightest. It verged on insanity, with his mouth curling up on one side and a few jagged teeth showing. And his eyes were beady, with one larger than the other. No one would give you such a thing as a present. Not unless they hated you.

And it wasn't as if Oscar could be ignored. Or shuffled off into a corner. He wasn't just big. He was enormous. You'd suffocate if he fell on you. Your last view of the world would be that evil leer.

'I won him,' Gladys added, 'in a raffle.'

Which was like winning a landmine. I turned to Kim, but she was no help. She was rarely stuck for words, but she seemed to be caught in a loop. 'Wow,' she said, peering up at the thing. 'Wow.'

'I went to Melbourne last Easter,' Gladys continued. 'You know I have family there. My son Bill and his wife Sarah and my grandchildren, Josh and Mona. Although they visit me, I don't like to put them out. They have busy lives, so I go to them—'

'But the panda—' I began.

'Goodness,' Gladys said, laughing. 'Am I prattling? Anyway, I bought a raffle ticket from some scouts in the city. Such lovely children. I was hoping to win a microwave oven or a Scrabble set. I do so love scrabble.'

'Let me make a guess,' I said. 'You didn't win either.'

'No! I won Oscar! I came home one day and found him on my doorstep. The scouts had dropped him off with a sign saying *My name is Oscar*. I couldn't even get him in the house. Actually, *I* couldn't even get in the *door*. He was blocking the entrance. It was my nice neighbour, Roger, who helped get Oscar inside. Actually, I told Roger he could have Oscar, but he said no.'

'Really,' I said. 'What a surprise.'

'He talks far too much for my liking.'

I stared at her. 'Oscar?'

'No!' Gladys stared at me as if I were crazy. 'Roger! He's a lovely man but a real chatterbox. Once he starts talking, he never stops.'

Now we had to work out how to get Oscar out of the house.

An image flashed through my mind of the Easter Island inhabitants working out a way to move their statues across the island. Ropes and pulleys were out of the question. So were UFOs and divine intervention seemed unlikely. A chainsaw set at high speed seemed the best solution, but that would defeat the purpose of our visit.

Kim and I grabbed an arm each and pulled. Oscar didn't move an inch, so I changed positions and seized his head while Kim gripped his legs.

'Oops!' Gladys shouted. 'Be careful of the flowers!'

Crash!

'Sorry about that!' I yelled.

'The bookcase!' Kim cried.

A pile of books were knocked to the floor. Something else broke. The pendant light from the ceiling swung crazily.

Oscar's arms seemed to have the unerring ability to grab everything within reach like a truculent child refusing to go to school. As I tried lifting Oscar up over the lounge, I only succeeded in falling over my own feet and ended up flat on my back, face to face with Oscar. He grinned evilly at me.

'Are you all right?' Kim asked from the far end of Oscar's anatomy.

'Peachy—' I gasped, shoving the stuffed panda away, '—keen!'

By angling Oscar around, we got him out the front door. Although, it wasn't without breaking a branch off a frangipani tree in the front yard and trampling over what turned out to be Gladys's prize-winning azalea.

Now for the next difficulty. I'd replaced my jeep's soft top with a hardtop. The back seat folded forward, which should have provided plenty of room, except Oscar didn't want to get into the car. We pushed and shoved as his pesky arms and legs flailed about in a desperate attempt to escape.

There's never an exorcist around when you need one!

After twenty minutes of shoving and pushing, we had most of him inside the vehicle, although his head and one arm still protruded crudely out the back window.

Oscar gave the impression he was either waving or struggling to break out.

And, still, he was smiling.

I was sweating and exhausted. Even Kim—my little fitness bunny friend—looked like she'd just fought twelve rounds against a crocodile. Gladys came to the driver's side window as I started the engine. 'Rosie,' she said. 'You'll look after him, won't you? This will sound strange, but…I've grown rather fond of him.'

Stockholm syndrome, I thought. *Can't be anything else.*

'He'll be looked after,' I assured Gladys, despite wanting to drive to the nearest headland to dump him in the ocean.

'He'll find a good home?'

'Oscar will be well looked after,' I promised.

Thanking Gladys for her donation, we headed down the street. We'd only gone three blocks, though, when I heard a siren behind us. I glanced in my side mirror and saw Cape Carson's most handsome police sergeant waving us down.

Pulling over, I turned to Kim. 'It's Todd,' I said. 'What does he want?'

'Maybe he wants to take Oscar home.'

'He's welcome to him.'

Todd sauntered over to the vehicle, quickly examining Oscar before stopping at my window. 'Rosie,' he said. 'Did you know there's a giant blue and pink stuffed panda sticking out the back of your vehicle?'

'Really? He wasn't there when I left for work this morning.'

'I can see you've made a valiant attempt to tie him up,' Todd said, ignoring me. 'But he seems to have made an escape attempt.'

I glanced back. Somehow, almost half of Oscar's body was now hanging out of the back of the vehicle. It was a shame he hadn't fallen out, and then we could have forgotten all about him.

'He's a naughty panda,' I said. 'We're taking him to the Sports Centre to be sold at Trash and Treasure.'

'I didn't think he was a hitchhiker,' Todd said, smiling. 'I'll shove him back in and give you a police escort.'

'That's very kind, but you don't need to—'

'The safest way, of course, will be straight down Percy Street.'

'Straight down…' My voice trailed away. 'But that's *the main road*.'

'Is it?' Todd's grin broadened. 'You follow me, and I'll get you and Kim and Godzilla—'

'Oscar.'

'—Oscar safely to the Sports Centre.'

He went to the boot and pushed as much of Oscar back in as possible before returning to his police vehicle.

'Maybe,' Kim began thoughtfully. 'I could get out here—'

'You're not going anywhere!'

Grimly, she settled back into the seat as I restarted the engine and followed Todd into town. He seemed to move at a snail's pace as he drove from one end of Percy Street to the other. People strolling down the road or sitting outside at cafes were greeted with the sight of Oscar waving at them as we passed. They stared. A French Bulldog started barking furiously. One man dropped his coffee.

Todd led us down to a roundabout and indicated right. He came around the roundabout—and headed back down Percy Street.

'You've got to be kidding,' I groaned.

We inched down Percy Street—again. This was obviously to catch people who'd missed the spectacle the first time. On this occasion, people were prepared and were taking photos. I shrunk down in my seat.

'Todd Parker,' I muttered. 'You'll be sorry...'

10

'Can't fault Leon for his marketing,' I said, reading the motto below the Cape Carson Panel Beaters sign. '*You bash 'em! We beat 'em!*'

'Certainly got a ring to it,' Kim agreed.

It was the next day, and we were following up on Leon's alibi for the day of his mother's death. His business was in a white-painted brick building next door to Cape Carson Auto Repairs on Hammond Street. The racket of engines and drills and grinding emanated from both places. I hadn't rung Leon to announce that we were visiting, preferring to catch him off-guard.

But Kim's attention was directed to the garage next door. 'Oh dear,' she said. 'I haven't been here for a while.'

Almost on cue, a man came out the front entrance, wiping his hands on a cloth as he headed for a car. He wasn't much taller than Kim but stockily built and prematurely balding. Spotting Kim, he smiled and made his way over.

'Hey Kimmy,' he said. 'Rosie.'

'Robert,' Kim said.

I felt for Kim. Robert Guest was Kim's ex-husband. He and Kim were more recently divorced than me. They'd broken up when Robert hired a new mechanic named Alex and decided he wanted to make a life with him rather than Kim.

Kim continued. 'How have you been?' she asked. 'And Alex?'

'We're good.' He glanced back at his garage. 'Come in and say hello.'

'I'd better not,' Kim said. 'We're busy.'

Robert glanced up at the panel beaters and my car. 'You're getting some work done on your jeep?' he said. 'Leon's one of the best around.'

'We're following up on the recent death of Leon's mum,' I explained.

'I heard about that. Fell down a flight of stairs, didn't she?'

'Over a balcony,' Kim said.

'What's Leon like?' I asked.

'He's got an explosive temper,' Robert said. 'Most of the time, you'd never see it. Although he's tough-looking, he's mostly quiet as a lamb. Unless someone pushes him the wrong way. Then he goes off like a rocket. Alex and I hear yelling. It's Leon screaming at one of his workers.'

Oh, dear. I wasn't looking forward to this meeting. Thanking Robert, Kim and I headed into Leon's workshop where we were hit by a wall of sound. Two men were grouped around a grinder. Another man was banging the frame of a vehicle with a mallet. The smell of grease, paint, and chemicals caught at the back of my throat.

Trixie sneezed, and I patted her head. 'It's okay, girl,' I said. 'This won't take long.'

Leon's office was near the front door. Windows ran along one side. He glanced up as we entered.

'Hello ladies,' he said, unable to stop a frown from momentarily creasing his forehead. 'I didn't expect to see you again. Need some work on your car?'

'Yes,' I said, laughing. 'But not right now. We're following up on something from the day your mum passed.'

The frown deepened. 'What is it?'

'Do you mind if we sit down?'

Leon grudgingly nodded.

I took the plunge. 'We were told that you were seen at her home the day she died,' I said.

'On Sunday?' Leon said. 'I was at work all day.'

'Really?' Kim said. 'Someone was pretty sure it was you.'

Anger flashed across Leon's face. 'I just said it wasn't me,' he said. 'I always visit Mum on Wednesdays. Anyone will tell you that.' He crossed to the door and yelled out. 'Johnno! Duck in here a minute, mate!'

A burly youth leaned into the office as Leon sat back down. 'Yeah, boss?'

'Where was I Sunday afternoon?'

Johnno thought. 'That was the day the old Ford arrived? The seventy-six?'

'The Ford Mustang?'

'That's it. You were here.'

'You sure about that? The whole day?'

'Sure. It was all hands on deck.'

Leon turned to us after the man left. 'You see,' Leon said, 'I was at work. Who's been telling stories about me?'

'I have to protect my sources,' I said automatically. However, my mind had been working, and I had another thought about this. 'I understand there was some animosity in your family.'

The panel beater shrugged. 'It's no big deal,' Leon said. 'Not to me, anyway. When Glenn and I were kids, mum and dad worked all the time. Dad had a building company, and we had no money. Half the time, they couldn't even pay their employees. Mum, Glenn, and I sometimes worked on building sites to keep us afloat. They were tough years.'

'That would cause some resentment.'

'Glenn and I wanted to be kids. We wanted to be out there driving cars and picking up girls. Instead, we were driving trucks and picking up timber. It was a hard life, but I don't care. It made me successful.'

'And Glenn?' Kim asked.

Leon hesitated. 'Glenn's always had a chip on his shoulder about it,' he said. 'Feels like he missed out on his childhood. I suppose he did. We both did. But there's no point crying over spilt milk. I don't deny that I used to get annoyed with Mum. She had dementia. She was hard to be around.'

Kim spoke up. 'Could it have been Glenn?'

I gave a small nod. The same idea had gone through my mind.

'Glenn?' Leon said. 'What do you mean?'

'The day your mum died,' Kim said. 'I'm wondering if the man who was seen was Glenn. You look alike. At a distance, someone could have mistaken you for your brother. It could have been him at the house the day she died.'

Leon sighed. 'I don't want to speak badly of Glenn,' he said. 'He's my brother, after all. But you can't think that he murdered mum?'

'We're just following up on a few loose ends,' I said. 'Do you think Glenn is capable of hurting someone?'

The man's jaw clenched. 'This is my brother we're talking about,' he said. 'I don't need to speak to you girls, and I've got a busy day ahead. I'd appreciate it if you left.'

Arguing was pointless. After politely thanking him, we returned to my jeep and got in. 'Something's going on here,' I said.

'Even Leon's wondering if Glenn could have attacked their mum,' Kim said, staring at the panel beaters. 'You could see it in his face.'

'Both men look similar,' I said. 'Vincent could have been mistaken when he said he saw Leon. It could have been Glenn.'

'Where to now?' Kim asked.

'Barkly. That's where Glenn's Salvage Yard is located.'

Trixie yowled and stuck her head between the two front seats. I slipped her a doggy snack. 'Don't you worry, girl,' I said. 'We'll go see this nasty man and then go for a long walk on the beach.'

She sat back, satisfied.

We drove north from Cape Carson.

It only took a few minutes to reach the outskirts of Barkly. Bush bordered the town. It was a tiny place with only a single row of shops surrounded by a few residential streets. The salvage yard was a ramshackle place at the end of one of the residential streets.

The corrugated iron fence surrounding the place was leaning badly. It needed repairing. The two wire gates were pushed back, allowing cars to enter, although there didn't seem to be any customers around. Littered about the inside were piles of second-hand building supplies.

Stacks of furniture lay everywhere, most faded and warped

by being left outdoors. At the back of the lot, nestled under gumtrees, sat an old demountable building that could have been a home or an office or both.

I stopped the car.

'What a great little business,' Kim said, peering out. 'Maybe we should invest.'

'Buy a lottery ticket instead,' I said. 'It's probably a safer bet.'

We climbed out and made our way to the office. There didn't seem to be anyone about, although an old ute was parked nearby. Leaning in the front door, I saw a desk, an old computer, and a chair. Paperwork lay everywhere.

An overflowing pile of crushed empty beer cans spilled from a large bin in the corner.

Trixie whined.

'You're right there, girl,' Kim said. 'This place smells bad.'

'I wonder where Glenn's gone.'

'Shopping?'

'Without his car? I doubt it.'

Rounding the desk, I glanced down at the papers. 'Wow,' I said. 'This doesn't look good. These are unpaid bills—lots of them.'

Kim looked about anxiously. 'Rosie,' she hissed. 'You can't just go reading people's personal papers!'

'I'm not,' I said innocently. 'I was worried that Glenn may have suffered a medical episode and needed our help.' My eyes narrowed on another stack of garishly coloured brochures. 'My goodness. These are travel leaflets. He's planning a holiday to Hawaii!'

'I suppose Glenn knows he's coming into money.'

'But these are old.' I gingerly picked one up by the corner. 'He's had this for months. He's been anticipating his mother's death.'

Kim frowned. 'Anticipating—or planning?'

His computer was unlocked so I could access his files. 'There's a setting in maps that shows your travel history,' I said. 'If I can find his movements for Sunday—'

A shadow filled the doorway. 'What—'

Glenn yelled and lurched around the desk as I scooted around the other side. He stared down at his computer, the paperwork, and brochures, before glaring at me with hatred in his eyes. 'What have you been doing?' he roared. 'Get out! Get out!'

Kim, Trixie, and I sprinted from the office and back to my jeep. Glenn wasn't far behind. As we piled in, he snatched up an iron bar and whacked the bar on the bonnet of my car as I started the engine. Although I yelled at him to stop, he seemed to grow further enraged. I put the vehicle in reverse and went veering backwards into a pile of timber. Trixie barked, and Kim screamed.

'He's out of control!' Kim cried. 'Drunk, crazy—'

'—and mad!' I yelled.

Glenn raced to his beat-up ute and jumped behind the wheel as I swung my jeep around and tore through the gates. I raced down the road, glancing in my rearview mirror.

'Is he following?' Kim asked.

The answer we got was his vehicle slamming into the back of my jeep.

I struggled to keep the car on the road and accelerated again. Up ahead, solitary farmhouses lined both sides of the road. Passing them, we reached a turn, and I rounded it, my wheels screeching. I accelerated again. I looked back in my mirror to see Glenn's ute attempt the same turn.

Almost as if in slow motion, I saw his car rise up on two wheels.

For a moment, I thought the vehicle would right itself. A better driver would have made it. Or a sober driver. But Glenn was neither. His car flipped sideways and landed in the ditch.

We drove back and clambered out. The wheels of Glenn's car were still turning and the engine running. Reaching his shattered driver's side door, I peered in and snapped off the ignition.

Glenn Spalt was alive, but his face was covered in blood.

Kim took out her phone and rang an ambulance as I spoke to Glenn.

She hung up. 'What did Glenn say?'

I sighed. 'Nothing that can be repeated,' I said. 'Maybe we can talk to him once he's cooled down.'

11

'Do you know how I spell Rosie?' Todd Parker asked. 'T-R-O-U-B-L-E.'

We were at Cape Carson hospital where Glenn Spalt had been admitted. Several hours had passed, during which Todd had interviewed both me and Kim.

'It's not all Rosie's fault,' Kim said. 'I was there too.'

'I know,' Todd said. 'You're as much to blame. It's just that Rosie is usually the ringleader.'

Trixie barked.

'See,' Todd said. 'Even Trixie agrees.'

'Todd,' I said, trying to keep the annoyance from my voice. 'We may have a strong lead.'

The big policeman sighed. 'Go ahead.'

I explained that a man fitting Glenn's description had visited his mum the day she died. We'd learned that the man wasn't Leon, so there was a good chance it was Glenn. Additionally, Glenn was deep in debt and had been planning an overseas holiday.

Todd shook his head. 'Girls—'

'Don't say we're imagining things!' I started.

'I'm not saying that. What I'm saying is that I'm already a step ahead of you.'

'Huh?' I stared at him. 'What do you mean?'

'I spoke to Leon after you visited him,' he said. 'Glenn was picking up furniture on Sunday afternoon.'

Kim asked. 'Are you sure it was him?'

'Absolutely. It was an old estate on the Coastal Road. I've checked with the people, and they described Glenn to a T.'

'But what about the travel brochures?' I asked. 'And the bills?'

'Rosie,' Todd said patiently. 'Glenn's obviously not the most financially stable guy around. You're right. He owes money all over the place. He's been waiting for his mother to die. But that's not a crime, no matter how distasteful it might sound. He's wanted to sell up and travel for years.'

I felt cheated. Surely someone who yelled at me, bashed my car with a lead pipe, and chased us down the street also had to be guilty of a million other things? Murder? Arson? Hurting small animals? 'All right,' I said, swallowing. 'Then there's Joe Porter's estate.'

'He may have been killed for his money,' Kim added.

'That's good reasoning,' Todd said. 'Which is exactly why I

looked into his case. And he had money. You know he won big on the lottery?'

'We know,' I said. 'So who inherits?'

'A niece named Kelly Porter. She grew up in Brisbane, but she's been living in Marble Bar in Western Australia for years. Joe Porter's solicitors have been in contact with her. It seems Kelly's never even met her uncle, let alone knew she was the beneficiary of his will.'

'Could the lawyers be mistaken?'

'We've checked her social media profile. You can find her online. She's legit. Once the house is sold, she'll get everything.' Todd's radio squawked. He sighed as he took a call about vandalism. 'That's it for me, ladies. Gotta go.'

We thanked him, and he headed off, leaving Kim and me to stare at each other.

'So this means that neither Glenn nor Leon were involved in their mother's death,' Kim said.

'And Joe Porter's only living relative lives out past the black stump,' I said.

'Which leaves us—where?' Kim asked. 'Back at square one?'

'No. We're back at our original theory: Joe Porter was killed by someone who hated him. Celia saw him die, and then the killer heard her at the Storytelling Tent and murdered her. The killer must be someone on the estate. We need to interview each of them.'

We wandered out into the car park, where I rang Harry at the office. The paper was going to print, and I needed to make sure everything was okay. He assured me that he and Jay had bulked up the paper with my other articles, and all was well. Hanging up, I felt a bit more relaxed. Harry was a great boss, and I never wanted to leave him in the lurch.

It was late in the day, and the sun was low in the sky. The high cloud was turning a brilliant shade of scarlet. A flock of King parrots burst squawking from a tree and went racing across the painted sky.

Kim and I stood and stared.

'Wow,' Kim said. 'That's quite a sight.'

'You're not wrong there.' My phone beeped, and I checked it. 'Oops. I'd better get going. I promised Amanda and Tom that I'd go for dinner. Do you have any plans? I'm sure they wouldn't mind if you tagged along.'

'I've got to do some serious reading for book club.'

We were both members of the Cape Carson Mystery Book Club, which met at our local library.

'Being the head librarian,' Kim continued, 'I should actually read the book.'

'You could do the same as me. I just make it up.'

'I don't have your creative flair.'

I dropped Kim off at her place in town before driving to Otway Street, where I lived with Nan. Dave Fisher was just turning into the driveway with her. She leaned out the window to wave.

'Hey girl,' she said. 'You joining us for dinner?'

'No. You two can canoodle together on the lounge in peace. I'm having dinner with Amanda and Tom.'

Trixie raced up to Nan as she got out of the car. Nan patted her head as she wandered over. 'While you're there,' she said, lowering her voice, 'you can ask that great-granddaughter of mine when she's having children.'

I'd been wondering the same thing. Tom and Amanda seemed so focused on their business that the topic of kids never seemed to come up. Still, I didn't feel it was my business to interfere. 'I don't think she's having any today,' I said. 'Maybe not even next week.'

'It's just that I'm not getting any younger.'

Dave strolled over and put his arm around her waist. 'You don't look a day over twenty-one to me,' he said.

'Keep those rose-tinted glasses on,' Nan said, smiling. 'They're working.'

We all headed inside. Dave was making one of his famous pastas for Nan. I went to my bedroom to change.

'Nan makes a good point,' I told Trixie. 'Tom and Amanda always seem to neatly sidestep the question of kids.'

Trixie barked.

'Ah,' I continued. 'So you've noticed it too. You're so

smart!'

I gave her a big hug before changing into a dress decorated with a frangipani flower print. It was a little old, but I could have turned up in a t-shirt and shorts, and Amanda and Tom wouldn't have minded.

Soon, I was knocking on their door, waving a good bottle of Shiraz in the other hand. Tom answered, smiling as he saw the bottle.

'You must have read my mind, Rosie,' he said. 'We're cooking lamb tonight.'

'Not so much mindreading, as ringing Amanda to see what I should bring.'

Tom was a clean-shaven guy with brown hair and eyes, and he looked young for his twenty-five years. Inside, Amanda was sitting at the dining room table, surrounded by piles of paperwork. Essentially, she was a more youthful version of me, but without my slightly Rubenesque body type.

'Hello, daughter,' I said, giving her a kiss and a hug. 'You're not bringing work home, are you?'

Amanda sighed. 'We've got two houses settling tomorrow, and we've just found out there's a caveat on one,' she said. 'And we're starting a new advertising campaign this week.'

Their business—Cape Real Estate—already ran regular ads with the Gazette. I remembered we were running a special double-page spread for them. It was twice their usual spend.

Amanda scooped up the paperwork. 'We're getting a lot of competition from that new agency.'

I frowned. 'What are they called? Carson Realty?'

'That's them. They're trying to entice clients with lower fees and big promises.'

'The real estate business is a people business,' I reminded her. 'You told me that.'

'Yes,' Amanda said, sighing. 'But money talks. Sometimes very loudly.'

She dropped the files on a coffee table and went to the kitchen to help Tom finish making the dinner. Within half an hour, we were seated around the table with glasses filled and enjoying his rosemary and garlic roast lamb. It was delicious, as usual. Tom didn't cook a lot, but he was good when he put his mind to it.

I mentioned that I hadn't seen them running lately.

'Running?' Amanda said. 'I enjoyed it. The old guy here hated it.'

'I didn't hate it!' Tom protested. 'It just made me too sweaty—and I've got to keep up a reputation as someone who doesn't sweat.'

'I'm sure real estate agents sweat,' I assured him, stifling a smile. 'So you're back rock climbing.'

They'd done a lot of rock climbing over the years. Although Tom had been climbing from when he was a boy, Amanda hadn't touched a rope or a carabiner until they met. Mostly they went climbing in the Tuxton Ranges, north of town, but they'd even gone as far as The Grampians and Mount Arapiles.

'We never stopped,' Amanda said. 'Our club's annual picnic is coming up next weekend. You can come if you want, mum.'

'Does it involve climbing?'

'Absolutely.'

'Then I'm swamped doing...something.'

They'd explained the safety procedures so often that I could virtually climb up and down a mountain myself. Not that I ever would. I loved mountains. Looking at them, at least. I'd happily leave the climbing to others.

I asked if they knew much about Sandcastle Village.

'We've sold a few properties there,' Amanda said, thinking. 'Tom, there was that woman—what was her name?'

'Naya,' Tom said. 'Naya Kapoor. She's a complete con artist.'

12

'Really?' I said. 'In what way?'

'She does some kind of online counselling and sells courses through her website about balancing your energies. Someone sued her a few years back. Something to do with a client who killed themselves.'

'Really?'

'Someone's wife, apparently. I heard the husband turned up at Sandcastle Village threatening blue murder. The cops were called in the end.'

So someone doesn't like Naya, I thought.

He stroked his chin. 'And there was Joe Porter, of course.'

'You knew him?'

'Only through selling him the house. He wouldn't stop telling us about how he'd won the lottery and was going to live it up big. Personally, I thought he'd end up bankrupt.'

Not bankrupt, I thought. *Worse than that—dead.*

I mentioned a few of the other people who lived on the

estate. The only one they knew was the antique dealer, Vincent Orr.

'We didn't sell him his place,' Amanda said. 'But we've heard stories.'

'Oh?'

She leaned close. 'Well,' she said. 'Everyone in business wants to make a profit. That's why they're in business. The problem with Vincent is that he's sold pieces that people thought were real, but were cheap knockoffs.'

'But that's fraud,' I said.

'There was fine print in the way the pieces were advertised. Someone tried to sue Vincent. Didn't get anywhere. Besides, Vincent comes across as a real charmer. He can turn it on when he wants.'

We'd finished dinner by now, and I helped Amanda clear the table. As we stacked the dishwasher, I mentioned what Nan had said about children.

'I wish she'd let up about that,' Amanda said, angrily stuffing cutlery into the dishwasher tray. 'We've been trying.'

'Okay,' I said carefully. 'No luck?'

'Not yet. We're even thinking about IVF. Anyway, we'll see what happens.'

I didn't want to press the point. After dinner, I thanked them for a great evening and headed home. Nan and Dave were still up watching TV. I wished them goodnight and went to my room, where Trixie took up her usual position on the floor.

'Doesn't look like I'll be a granny anytime soon,' I told her.

She sunk her head down onto her front paws.

'It's okay,' I said. 'Everything in its time.'

The following day, I decided to return to Sandcastle Village. Still in bed, I rang Kim to see if she was available.

'I sure am,' she said, sounding terribly cheerful. 'I'm just about ready for coffee.'

'Where are you?'

'Up near Cut Rock. I've been running.'

'Really?' I said. Kim was an avid runner. Exercise made no sense to me. Why go for a run when you could sit in bed with tea and biscuits, and read a book instead? 'Were you being chased by a psycho in a hockey mask?'

'No, but I'd date just about anyone.'

'I'll meet you at Sandy's.'

Half an hour later, I was seated out the front of Sandy's Diner. Although the months were getting colder, this morning's sky was crisp and the bay flat. A fishing boat rounded the breakwater and arrowed for the dock. Two squawking seagulls landed near my feet. Trixie gave a single bark, and they flew off.

I laughed. 'You showed them who's boss.' She burrowed her head against my knee, and I gave her one of my homemade Trixie snacks. 'Smoocher!'

Kim came trotting down the footpath and sat down. 'Were

you waiting long?'

'Hardly any time at all.' I stared at her. 'Did you go home and change?'

'Sure. Everything's easier when you run.'

'I'm sure everything is…except…well…running.'

Kim had seen some whales far out at sea as she'd passed the lighthouse. This was whale watching season and one of my favourite times of the year.

Sandy Clementine appeared, notepad in hand. She was a buxom woman with short-cropped blonde hair and tattoos on both arms. 'Morning chickadees,' she said. 'You having breakfast? Or just surviving on coffee?'

Kim had already eaten, and I'd jammed a piece of toast down my throat before leaving the house. We ordered takeaways: my usual jumbo double-shot caramel latte for me and a skim cappuccino for Kim. I peered more closely at Sandy's arm.

'Is that a new tattoo?' I asked.

'It sure is. I had the first line of Buddy Holly's *True Love Ways* added.'

She already had over a dozen lines of musical notes and words from songs on her arms. Although I'd never been into tattoos myself, I thought they looked good on some people.

'Nice,' I said.

Sandy got us our takeaway coffees, and we went to my car where Trixie settled down in the back seat.

'Who are we speaking to first?' Kim asked.

'I'm not sure.' I took a long sip of my caramel latte, and my brain exploded with joy at the perfect blend of sugar and caffeine. 'Maybe whoever we run into.'

We soon arrived at the gated community. I pulled into Doris's driveway. Sandcastle Village seemed strangely quiet, although it was still early in the day. People may have gone out or, as some did, could be working from home. The only person in sight was Vincent's son, Graham, sitting on his front step. It looked like he was killing ants with a magnifying glass.

We got out of my car.

'What a hideous child,' I muttered.

Kim frowned. 'If reincarnation is real,' she replied, 'I hope he comes back as an ant.'

'Do you believe that stuff?'

'My second cousin Melanie thought she had once been Marie-Antoinette. She swore blind it was the reason for her sore neck on cold mornings.'

We made our way up the front path with Trixie. 'You must be Graham,' I said, forcing a smile. 'How old are you?'

The boy looked sulky. 'Twelve,' he said. 'Why do you want to know?'

'Just curious.' He was taking up most of the front step and wasn't in a hurry to move. 'We'd like to speak to your dad.'

'About what?'

'About some stuff. Can we get past?'

'You have to say the magic word.'

There were a few magic words I felt like saying, although none were the type that should be used in front of a child. Fortunately, the front door cracked open at that moment, and Vincent appeared. He flung his arms wide.

'Ladies!' he said. 'Welcome to our humble home. Graham, move out of the way so these lovely ladies can pass. And bring in your beautiful dog!'

Graham reluctantly shuffled aside, and we strode past him into a cool, dark house that was crowded with antiques and precious items. Oak sideboards lined the walls. Bookshelves jammed several rooms. Tables and chests of drawers crammed against each other. The place was so packed with things that I had no idea where to look. It was more like an overstocked showroom than a home.

'What a beautiful house,' Kim said politely. 'You obviously love antiques.'

'It's a lifelong obsession,' Vincent enthused. 'The biggest problem is when you fall in love with things and can't bear to let them go.' We settled into a lounge while Vincent fetched some water. Trixie sat nearby, looking as intimidated as I felt.

'So you'd like to know all about Sandcastle Village,' Vincent said as he poured drinks and settled down opposite. 'Well, you've come to the right place. I've been here longer than most people.'

'How long have you lived here?' I asked.

'Nine years.'

'And it's just you and your son?'

Vincent hesitated. 'I'm divorced,' he said. 'My wife left us—left *me*—to raise our son alone.' He forced a smile. 'The whole episode scarred Graham most terribly. He adored his mother, and then she just walked out on us one day and never returned. He still hasn't recovered.'

'Someone mentioned that you home school Graham?'

'He needs individual attention. His therapist agrees.'

Kim spoke up. 'I've seen you at the library,' she said.

Vincent smiled. 'I love your rare book collection. Some date to the nineteenth century.' He nodded to several volumes on a nearby shelf. 'I've got a few of my own, as you can see.'

'Talking about stories, we had Celia Spalt at our Storytelling Tent last Saturday.'

'She died the next day,' I prompted.

'Oh yes. I saw Glenn visiting her. You remember me saying?'

'We chatted to Glenn. He denies seeing his mother.'

Vincent rubbed his chin. 'I could be wrong,' he admitted. 'It was someone in overalls. It could have been a gardener, but they come every third Monday. And I don't know why they'd be knocking at Celia's door. They normally look after the footpaths and the park. They have no reason to visit the residents.'

I stroked Trixie's back. 'You had another death here a while back,' I said. 'Joe Porter.'

'Oh, him!' Vincent laughed. 'What a repulsive man. I don't wish to speak ill of the dead, but no one liked him.'

'Really?'

'He argued with everyone. You've probably already heard about Joe's big lottery win. He used to flaunt it all the time. You can't help but dislike someone who shows off their wealth. It's unseemly. And Joe may have been rich, but he was small-minded. He developed grudges against people over the smallest of things.'

'When you say grudges...' Kim began.

'Well, my yard for one. I used to have a border of the loveliest roses, including a whole line of Madame Anisettes and Mister Lincolns. Took me years to grow. They were stunning. Then I saw Joe cutting some off. He wanted them for his home! I challenged him on it. I mean, if he'd asked, I may have given him some, but—'

'What did he say?' I interrupted.

'He seemed surprised that I was upset! Can you imagine it? We got into a rather loud exchange—and then he walked off.' Vincent shuddered. 'I should have known that wouldn't be the end of it. A few weeks went by. Then one morning, I noticed my roses were wilting, and the grass was yellowing. Someone had sprayed poison all over the lawn and garden.'

'Good grief. Did you ask Joe about it?'

'I did—although I knew it would be a waste of time. Joe denied everything. Said people were always blaming him for things.' A flash of fury crossed Vincent's face. He forced it away. 'Joe was lying, but I knew. I'm sure everyone on the estate can tell you similar stories. No one likes to speak ill of the dead, though I doubt you'll find many who speak well of Joe Porter. Now, onto other subjects.' He took a notepad from his pocket. 'Let me tell you about the advantages of living here at Sandcastle Village. I've made a list.'

As he reeled off the estate's high points, I thought what he'd said about his garden. Would someone kill their neighbour for destroying their plants? People had been killed for lesser reasons.

I made a few notes as Kim took pictures.

We thanked Vincent and returned to the street. Wandering back to my car, I asked Kim her thoughts.

'You saw that look of anger?' she said. 'He was furious. I wouldn't want to be on the wrong side of that in an argument.'

'I suppose everyone gets angry sometimes.'

'There's anger,' Kim said. 'And then there's rage. He could have killed Joe, and maybe Celia saw it—ouch!' She spun around as a pebble bounced onto the ground. 'That hit my head!'

Trixie let out an angry bark, and I quietened her. We stared at Vincent's house. There was no sign of movement. Then I spotted something shuffling amongst the bushes: Graham disappeared around the side of the house.

'That little brat!' I snapped. 'We should wring his neck!'

'Don't waste your energy. The kid's obviously deranged.' She rubbed her head. 'What now?'

A car pulled into the driveway of Trudi Kendrix's house, and the attractive blonde climbed out.

'Let's chat to Trudi,' I said. 'We'll see if she hated Joe Porter too.'

13

'I remember you,' Trudi said as we approached. 'You two were at the funeral. You're doing a story about the estate?'

'We'd love to get your perspective on Sandcastle Village.'

Trudi glanced at her watch. 'I can spare you a few minutes,' she said. 'Then I've got to get on with things.'

Her home was sparse to the point of being barren. The walls and floor were concrete with highlights of stained timber. I'd seen this done before and thought it looked attractive. This time it bordered on sterile.

Not one for decorations, I thought.

'What a lovely place,' Kim said, glancing at me.

'Thanks,' Trudi said. 'I like it. I love your dog, by the way. Beagles are so friendly.' She showed us to her living room and waved us into lounge chairs. 'So you'd like to know about the Village.'

'Yes, please,' I said.

She explained that she'd lived there for about five years.

Because Trudi was employed as a programmer, she could work from home.

Besides her work, she'd bought into a fintech company a few years before and made a lot of money. It allowed her to buy the house in Sandcastle Village.

'I know an article about the estate will raise house prices,' she said, 'but I don't really need the money. I've done all right for myself.'

'So you're working now?' Kim said.

'There's a project I'm doing for an Adelaide start-up.' The woman's face fell. 'It's something new. I was fired from my last job.'

'I'm sorry to hear that.'

'It wasn't my fault, mind you. And you can probably guess who was to blame.'

I exchanged glances with Kim. 'Joe Porter?' I guessed.

'You got it.' Trudi sighed. 'I should have expected it. Anyone who crossed Joe Porter met with 'bad luck'. I made the mistake of complaining about his rubbish. You see, Joe would dump things out in front of his house.'

Trudi shrugged. 'I mean, seriously, who did he think would clean up that stuff? Rubbish is supposed to be binned and left outside the front gates. Instead, he'd leave boxes containing all kinds of junk outside his home: broken radios, lamps, license plates, chunks of wood.'

'So, one day, I challenged him on it. Said he couldn't leave his junk on the footpath. Anyway, there was quite an argument. Olivia and Henry Rudd came out to see what was going on and calmed everyone down. They're the peacemakers of this place. Dear Olivia picked up the box and took it away in the end.'

Trudi examined her nails. 'Of course,' she said, 'I was naïve. I didn't know what I'd started. The next thing I knew, my name and personal details were plastered on websites everywhere. They said I was a neo-Nazi—and worse. Hate mail began to arrive.' Her face clouded over. 'It was Joe's doing, of course, and my employer found out. At first, they were sympathetic, but then it began to impact their business. They let me go.'

Trixie sat her head on my knee, and I rubbed her back. 'Was Joe that tech-savvy?' I asked.

'He was no dummy, and he had time on his hands. When you're retired with lots of money, you can sit around and plot all kinds of evil.'

'And now Celia's died.'

'It was bound to happen sooner or later. Everyone liked Celia, although she barely made sense half the time. The person I feel for is Violet. She was her constant companion.' She leaned close. 'Some might say closer than a friend, but I don't care. What people do in their own homes is their business. Either way, Violet put in the hours, and it must have been *really* tough putting up with Celia.'

'Violet sometimes had to leave Celia at home,' Kim said. 'So she could go out and shop.'

Trudi shrugged. 'I don't blame her,' she said. 'Neither of her sons would help. Glenn was useless, and Leon was downright hostile towards his mother.'

I tried to sound casual. 'Were you here when Celia died?'

'No,' Trudi replied, glancing at her watch. 'I was getting my nails done.'

'At Judy's?'

'That's right. Lyla, her daughter, does a wonderful job.'

Half the women in town went to Judy's Hair and Nails. I reminded myself to check Trudi's alibi with her.

'Look,' the woman continued. 'I hate to kick you out, but I've got to work. I have an online meeting in fifteen minutes, and I need to fix my hair.'

We thanked her and returned to the street.

'Goodness,' I said. 'That was quite a tale. I once did a story about a woman whose ex-husband ruined her life by plastering her personal details all over the internet. She got death threats and hate mail for years. Eventually, the woman had to change her name and move to a new town.'

'That's terrible.'

I was about to suggest we return to Sandy's for another coffee when I spotted Olivia and Henry Rudd emerging from the park. I gave them a wave. Although the man smiled, the woman looked at us vaguely as we crossed.

'Hello,' I said, beaming at them. 'You're Olivia and Henry?'

The man frowned. 'We are. Are you visiting someone?'

He was obviously worried about security. Explaining that we were friends with Doris, I gave them our cover story.

'Oh, I see,' Henry said. 'Well, I don't know if we have much to say. Sandcastle Village is lovely. The neighbours are friendly. It's safe. The whole place runs like clockwork.'

Although he seemed eager to be on his way, I needed to keep him and Olivia talking. 'And you?' I said, turning to her. 'What do you think?'

Until now, Olivia's focus had been on Henry, but now she looked past me as if staring at a distant point. Her eyes creased as if the light were painful. 'I like it very much,' she said. Olivia had a broach—a gold angel—that she wore on her cardigan. She touched it unconsciously as she spoke. 'The people are nice. I like all our neighbours. Especially now that Joe Porter's gone.'

'My dear,' Henry said. 'We mustn't speak like that. We don't want to give these women the wrong impression.'

'But he was a terrible man, and the angels took revenge.'

I wasn't sure I'd heard her correctly. 'The angels?'

'There are forces at work beyond our senses.'

'Maybe we could sit down and chat,' Kim suggested.

An expression of sheer panic crossed Henry's face. 'No,' he said. 'I don't think—'

'That would be lovely,' Olivia cut in. 'Come for tea. And bring your dog.'

'My dear—' Henry started again.

Olivia's voice rose sharply. 'These women can come for tea! And their dog! We need visitors. We hardly see anyone.'

Henry Rudd obviously knew his wife well enough to know when to surrender. 'Of course, my dear,' he said. 'These ladies can come for tea, as long as they have time.'

We assured him we did. Neither Olivia nor Henry spoke as we made our way to their place.

Henry seemed like a jackrabbit ready to bolt, and there was no knowing what was going through Olivia's head.

They led us through the front door and showed us into a well-appointed living room. Olivia asked if we'd like tea and biscuits, and a few minutes later, we were all nursing cups around the coffee table.

'I'm not sure what we can tell you about living here,' Henry began. 'It's like any other place, really. We get up in the morning, go out and do some shopping. We live quiet lives. Do a lot of reading. Jigsaw puzzles. Watch TV.'

'You're retired?' I asked.

'I was a professor at Melbourne University, where I taught Business Analytics.'

I turned to Olivia. 'And you?'

'I was a bookkeeper. Both Henry and I are numbers people.'

Kim smiled. 'Numbers have never really been my thing.'

'They appeal to me,' Henry continued, 'because numbers are either right or wrong. There's no messiness, unlike the humanities. A much more difficult subject, in my opinion.'

'And have you lived here long?' I asked.

The pair had purchased their land when Sandcastle Village was still being built. They were the first people to move in, with Vincent and his family moving in soon after. There'd been some turnover of households since then. The most recent addition was Joe Porter.

Olivia's face clouded over. 'We had terrible arguments with him,' she said petulantly. 'He was a nasty man.'

Henry swallowed. 'Olivia,' he said. 'We need to watch our words.'

'He hit you! He should not have done that!'

This was news to me. 'Joe Porter hit you?' I said to Henry. 'My goodness. What happened?'

The ex-professor's face reddened. 'Joe Porter was somewhat of a peeping tom.'

'What?' Kim said. 'That's terrible.'

'He owned binoculars and would watch everyone from his front room. Most people didn't know he was there. We could see him because of the angle of our window. His curtain was translucent, and we saw him spying on people.'

Olivia piped up. 'Henry confronted him!' she said. 'He knocked on Joe's door and told him to stop.'

'What did Joe say?' I asked.

'He said Henry was crazy,' Olivia said. 'Said he should mind his own business.'

Henry continued. 'I'm afraid one thing led to another. Joe reeked of alcohol. There was some pushing and shoving. We had a bit of a tussle before I marched off in a huff. I told Joe I'd report him to the police for starting a fight, although I never did.'

'Why not?'

'What's the point? We all have to live here together.'

'And higher powers enable justice,' Olivia cut in. 'Forces beyond our own mete out punishment—'

'Olivia,' Henry pleaded.

She fell to silence. Trixie went to her, and Olivia stroked her back.

'Someone told us that Joe was difficult in other ways, too,' Kim said. 'Underhanded.'

'I didn't know that at the time, although I discovered it soon enough. It happened after our argument. We owned a cat: Napoleon, his name was. Anyway, one day he was here, the next he was gone. We never saw him again.'

Olivia was staring into the distance. 'Dear Napoleon,' she

said. 'We did love him so. Napoleon's with the angels now. And then Joe would leave his rubbish out on the footpath. One day he left a box of junk out there—'

'Olivia!' Henry snapped. 'We don't want to hear about that box again.'

His wife looked at him, her chin quivering. At first, I thought she would burst into tears. Then she slammed her cup onto the table. Trixie yelped. 'We've already been through enough!' she said. 'There are angels everywhere! The power is in their hands!'

She marched from the room, and a door slammed shut a few seconds later. Trixie came back and settled beside me.

'I must apologise,' Henry said, putting down his cup. 'Olivia's a bit high strung. Our son died several years ago, and she's never been the same.'

'I'm so sorry,' I said.

'Her family was very religious growing up, and now she sees angels and omens in everything.'

'I see.'

Henry changed the subject and talked about Celia, saying her death wasn't entirely a shock. She'd grown more confused over the last year and often wandered. Once or twice, she'd even ended up in other people's backyards.

'We found her in our shed one time,' Henry said, shaking his head. 'Poor dear. Had no idea where she was. Said she was looking for her bedroom. I took her back home to Violet.'

He continued to speak, but I couldn't stop thinking about Olivia. I wondered what she meant by saying *the power is in their hands*.

Asking if I could use the bathroom, Henry directed me, and I headed down a hallway. I popped in for a couple of minutes before returning to the hall. Olivia was in a sitting room at the other end, staring into space.

I leaned in the door. 'I hope we didn't upset you,' I said. 'I'm sorry if we did.'

'It's all right.' The woman didn't move. 'I'm easily upset.'

On the table beside her was a photo of a young boy. 'Is that your son?'

Olivia's eyes angled to the picture. 'That's our boy, Simon,' she said. 'My beautiful boy.'

'He's handsome.'

The woman smiled sadly. 'He looked more like his father than me,' she said. 'Probably for the best.'

I waited.

'He was killed in a hit and run about eighteen years ago this October,' Olivia continued. 'He was only nine. A good boy. Simon was crossing the road at a pedestrian crossing, like I always told him, when a car came through and ran him down.' Her eyes turned to me. 'Do you have children, Rosie?'

'A daughter.'

'Hold her close,' she said. 'You never know what's around the corner.'

I nodded. 'You mentioned angels. Can you tell me more?'

Olivia looked past me. 'No,' she said. 'Henry doesn't like me talking about them. And I'm tired now. I tire easily these days. You'll like Sandcastle Village. If you live here long enough, you'll see angels too.'

14

I told Kim what Olivia had shared with me as soon as we reached the footpath.

'The poor woman's mad,' Kim said sympathetically. 'She's never recovered from her son's death.'

'Then she needs a doctor.' I peered at the house. 'Henry probably means well, but hiding her away from the world can't be helping.'

My phone rang: Nan.

'Rosie!' she said as soon as I answered. 'Are you busy?'

'You mean apart from doing my job?'

'Great! I've got another pickup for Trash and Treasure.'

I groaned. 'Really, Nan?' I said. 'Can't you find someone else?'

'This'll be easier than last time.' I'd told Nan about parading Oscar up and down the main road of Cape Carson. 'It's just someone's collection of ornaments.'

Well, that sounded easy enough. 'All right,' I relented.

'Can you go now?'

'Now? Why?'

'The husband's in some kind of hurry.'

Grumbling, I agreed to head there immediately. Nan gave me the details, and soon Kim and I were pulling up in front of a house on the west side of town. The place sat nestled beneath some flowering wattle trees. I knocked on the front door.

It creaked open, and an elderly man appeared.

'John?' I said.

His face brightened. 'You're the Trash and Treasure girls?'

'That's us,' Kim said brightly. 'I'm Trash.'

'And I'm Treasure,' I added, laughing.

He stared at us.

'Just a little Trash and Treasure comedy,' I continued feebly. Clearly, he'd been born without a sense of humour. 'I understand you're donating some ornaments?'

'Oh yes,' he said, glancing back into the house. 'Just keep your voices down. My wife Maureen's asleep. It's her clown collection.'

'Clowns?' Kim's face fell. 'Did you say...clowns?'

'She's got a lot,' John said. 'Been collecting for years.'

He opened the door. I followed him down the hallway with Trixie as Kim trailed behind. The living room was a carnival of colours. Over a thousand clown ornaments lined the shelves and display cabinets. They seemed to come in every shape and size. The smallest was only a few inches high, the biggest almost a foot. Most were white and red and blue, although a few were odd shades of yellow and green. The clowns were in every possible pose: standing, singing, dancing, running, or swaying. A lot were balancing on one leg, an arm. A few were even upside down. Most appeared to be ceramic, although some were plastic and a couple were metal.

As collections went, it was quite impressive. The old man had considerately brought in a few packing boxes to take them away in, but it was clear we'd need more. I asked if he had any.

'There's some down the back,' he said. 'I'll get them. Just keep your voices down.'

He headed out, leaving me alone with Kim, Trixie, and the thousand clowns. I peered around at the collection. A lot of people collected knickknacks. Nan liked ceramic mice; a few dozen sat around the house. I knew another lady who had over two hundred koalas. It was nice to have hobbies.

This would make for a good news story.

'What an amazing collection.' I turned to Kim, who was pale and leaning against the wall. 'Kim! Are you all right?'

'Rosie,' she groaned, dragging me back into the hallway. 'There's something I've never told you. But we've been friends a long time. Can I tell you something silly?'

'It's never stopped you before. What is it?'

'Clowns.' Her face was filled with dread. 'I can't stand

them.'

I glanced about. 'But clowns are fun,' I said. 'They're happy, and they dance, and they—'

'No,' Kim said, emphatically shaking her head. 'For other people, maybe. For me, it's like walking into a nightmare. Everyone's got their Achilles Heel. Superman's got kryptonite. Indiana Jones is scared of snakes. Popeye needs his spinach. Clowns are my Achilles Heel.'

'Really?'

'You probably thought I was indestructible until now.'

'Well, no, actually—'

'But the truth is that I'm terrified of clowns. I can't stand them. If you were to ask me why I don't like them, I could give you a million reasons, and none would make sense.' Horror filled her eyes as she gazed from one clown to another. 'Clowns dress funny. They wear oversized shoes and colourful onesies. They make jokes. Pull pranks. They do acrobatics. Sing and dance. Clowns *clown* around.'

'Uh, that's kinda their job.'

'But what are they thinking? Rosie—they're *always* smiling! *Always!*' A line of sweat drained down the side of Kim's face as she stared at me, wide-eyed. 'What are they *plotting* beneath that smile? Murder? Revolution? A clown apocalypse?'

'So you've got a fear—'

'You know what that is? A *clownaclypse!*'

'That's not a real word—'

She gripped my arm, and Trixie whined. 'You know that a fear of clowns even has a name?' she said. '*Coulrophobia*.'

'Uh, yes.' I peered at her worriedly. Kim had turned quite red. I didn't want her passing out or ending up in hospital. We had a thousand clowns to box up, and I couldn't do it alone. 'Kim,' I said gently. 'This is too big a job for me.'

'Rosie. I'd go to Hell and back for you. I'd jump from a moving train. I'd wrestle a crocodile.'

'I wouldn't expect you to wrestle a crocodile—'

'But *clowns*.' She shuddered. 'There's only so much a girl can take.'

This was wild, particularly coming from the woman who loved horror films. How often had she tried to get me to watch The Exorcist? Or a late-night viewing of Evil Dead? Or The Omen? And now it turns out that she's scared of *clowns*?

'Kim. I *need* your help.'

My friend swallowed. She peered back at the room and reached a decision. 'Rosie,' she said. 'You know I'd never let you down.'

'Thanks, Kim—'

'But this time, you're on your own.'

She scooted down the hallway and disappeared outside. I turned back just as John reappeared with some more boxes.

'Your friend's gone?' he said.

'Getting some fresh air.'

'Funny. That happens a lot when people come to visit. Some people don't like clowns. Did you know that?'

'So I've heard.'

I started doggedly boxing up clowns. John apparently wasn't interested in helping either, so he vanished back out to his shed. It didn't take long for me to develop my own aversion to clowns. Having to singlehandedly box up a thousand of them will cool you to their charms.

Trixie sat in the corner and watched.

'Are you going to help?' I asked.

She whined.

'You too?' I grumbled. 'We're never going to the circus again.'

An hour passed as I boxed up the ornaments. Once I got into a rhythm, it didn't take long. I gradually ferried the boxes outside, where Kim gingerly took possession and packed them into the back of my jeep. It was a tight squeeze, but we got them all in. Just as we were ready to drive off, John raced up to the driver's side window.

'Girls,' he said urgently. 'Maureen's woken up, and she's not happy.'

'Uh, why?' I asked.

John looked embarrassed. 'Well, to tell you the truth, I didn't actually tell her that I was getting rid of her collection.'

'*What?*'

'They stop my sister Marj from visiting!' He looked pained. 'She won't even step foot in the place!'

A woman burst from the house like a banshee. This was obviously Maureen, fresh from her nap but now ready to confront whoever had stolen her beloved clown collection. Her white hair was unkempt and wild. She wore a nightgown covered in red and blue dots and giant flip-flop slippers. Before going to bed, the woman had neglected to remove her make-up, so her bright red lipstick was smudged, her eyeliner was smeared, and her cheeks were crimson with anger.

Kim shrank back in terror. 'Oh no!' Kim gasped. 'She's a *clown*!'

'No,' I said. 'No...I mean—'

The woman reached the car. 'What are you doing?' she shrieked. 'What have you done with my clowns?'

I summonsed up all my years of journalistic experience. 'Um,' I said. 'Um.'

Was she furious with me? Or John? It couldn't be Kim. She'd sunk down so low in her seat she was almost out of view. Even Trixie had ducked out of sight. John fell back in fear, leaving me in no doubt as to who ruled the roost. Even I was terrified of Maureen, and I was able-bodied, a foot taller, and thirty years younger.

John reddened. 'Well, dear,' he stammered. 'The time has

come for them to go to a new home.'

'*What?*' Her eyes shot to the boxes in the back. 'Are you *mad*? This is twenty years of my life! How dare you steal my clowns!' She slammed her fist on the bonnet. 'Let them go! Give them back!'

I wasn't sure what to do. Staring at John wasn't helping. He was frozen to the spot. Then he seemed to reach a final, dramatic decision as his eyes turned to mine.

'Go!' he yelled. 'Go!'

I swerved the car, slamming my foot on the accelerator, and took off down the street. I peered back in the rearview mirror to see Maureen staggering after us. Not until we turned the corner did I glance over at Kim, still crouched in the passenger seat.

'Kim?' I said. 'Are you all right?'

At first, I thought she was catatonic. Then she eased back up in her seat and turned to me. 'Clowns,' she muttered. '*Not* funny.'

15

I lingered outside the Cape Carson Public Library with two coffees in hand for almost five minutes before gathering up the courage to enter. Hattie Kale, a young woman with a big batch of red hair, was at the front desk. I greeted her before peering past into Kim's office where she was working.

Kim glanced up. Much to my relief, a smile crossed her face. She waved me in, I sat down opposite and slid a coffee over to her.

'All okay?' I asked.

'Of course. I'm sorry about yesterday.'

'Me too. That went kind of pear-shaped.'

We'd only just started unpacking the boxes at the Sports Centre when John had turned up in his car and asked us to return the clown collection.

It turned out that Maureen's wrath was too much to bear. She'd threatened to leave him if the clowns weren't returned. Personally, if I had to choose between Maureen and the clowns, I'd prefer the clowns, but each to their own. The worst part of it was Kim's trauma. When I'd dropped her at home, she'd gotten out of the car without even saying goodbye.

'It's a phobia,' Kim said. 'I can't explain it.'

'No explanation necessary. We've all got irrational fears.'

Trixie sat her head on Kim's knee. 'Really?' she said. 'You've got an irrational fear? What is it?'

'Um, some other time.' I pressed on, not keen to reveal my deepest darkest secret at this point in time. 'Are you okay if we chat about where we're at with the investigation?'

'Just so long as Ronald MacDonald isn't a suspect.'

'He's not,' I assured her and took a long sip of my coffee. 'Okay. Let's look at Celia's death. Hannah spotted someone she thought was a gardener on the day Celia died. Vincent also saw someone going to Celia's door, whom he described as wearing overalls. They could have been a gardener, except it was the wrong day and the wrong week for the gardeners.'

'A gardener would have no reason to murder Celia. So it was someone who usually wore overalls or someone pretending to be a gardener.'

'Exactly. The most likely suspects are Glenn or Leon, except they both have alibis.'

'And we know that Celia was probably killed because she witnessed a murder.'

'Absolutely. That opens up the whole suspect pool. Which

means it could be anyone who lives on the estate. One of them disguised themselves as a gardener to commit the crime.' I paused. 'For that matter, it could also be someone who lives *off* the estate. A visitor to the estate could have killed Joe and then heard Celia at the Storytelling Tent. It's easy enough to gain entry by tailgating someone into Sandcastle Village.'

'True,' Kim agreed. 'But we can't start chasing up everyone who lives outside the estate because that's basically the whole planet.' She sipped her coffee. 'I've been thinking about that kid.'

'Graham Orr? He is *very* odd.'

'*And* he threw a rock at me,' Kim grimaced. 'Of course, that doesn't make him a killer. Just a delinquent child.'

'Though he could be one of those child killers. He murdered Joe because he disliked him and then killed Celia because she saw him do it.'

'So we can't rule him out as a suspect. Who else have we got?'

'His father, Vincent. He may have murdered Joe for revenge over his garden.'

'All right. Who else?'

I thought for a moment. 'Trudi, obviously. She disliked Joe because he ruined her reputation and got her fired. And Hannah. Joe Porter tried to poison her dog. Then there's Henry and Olivia Rudd. Henry had a physical fight with Joe Porter. And Olivia...' I sighed. 'That poor woman is unwell.'

'Olivia is odd,' Kim agreed. 'But there's a problem here. Henry had a fight with Joe Porter, Trudi was fired because of him, Hannah's dog almost got poisoned, and Vincent had his garden ruined. But are they reasons to kill someone? You can understand a crime of passion. Something that happens on the spur of the moment. But Joe Porter was apparently on a walk through the park when someone hit him over the head. And the same person murdered an old lady.'

'In a way,' I said, 'Celia's death is easier to understand. She was murdered to cover up the first crime. But I agree. These are fairly flimsy murder motives. We're talking about actually taking a person's life. That's usually a crime of revenge. Or passion. Or greed. And none of this explains the 'gardener' that both Vincent and Hannah saw on the day of Celia's death.' This was all too much. There were too many suspects and motives, and none of it was making sense. I peered up at Kim. 'Do you have time for a few more interviews? Please? I know we're potentially speaking to a killer...'

Kim laughed. 'Are you kidding?' she said. 'I faced a thousand clowns yesterday. I can handle *anything* after that.'

Half an hour later, we were back at Sandcastle Village and knocking on the door of Naya Kapoor. A moment later, the door swung open to reveal the woman standing there in a flowing indigo-coloured chiffon gown. Her eyes lit up. 'Ah,' she said, with only the faintest of Indian accents. 'The girls from the newspaper.' She knelt and patted Trixie, her eyes shifting to Kim. 'Although I think you work at the library.'

'I do,' Kim said. 'I also help with the paper's photography.'

'I've been to your library—and I'm disappointed. You don't have my book in stock.'

'Your book?'

'Come inside, and I'll show you.'

We followed her into a house that smelt strongly of incense. A buddha sat on a pedestal in the living room. Middle-eastern rugs and tapestries covered the floors and walls. A water fountain flowed in the corner. The faint sound of recorded birdsong filled the air.

Naya went to a nearby bookcase. 'Here,' she said. 'I can give you a copy for your collection.'

Kim took it and we read the cover.

'*Only You Can Make it Happen*,' I said. 'That sounds very...transformational.'

'That's what I do,' Naya smiled, revealing a row of perfectly white teeth. 'I transform lives. Help people to get to where they want to go.'

'You're a psychologist?'

'A psychotherapist. These days I practice mostly online. I can reach more people that way.' She waved us into seats and grabbed us some water to drink. 'I only drink water in the mornings. It keeps my energies aligned.'

'I see.'

'Of course, you want to know about our wonderful home: Sandcastle Village. It's a special place.' She breathed in deeply. 'I can tell when a place has a good vibration. You know that places have vibrations? Just like people. Harmonious lives are created when we all vibrate on the same frequency.'

I nodded.

'Sandcastle Village has such a vibration. From the moment you enter the gates, you know that you're in a place of peace.'

'Oh, yes.' I didn't speak again until she had handed out drinks and sat down. Trixie settled at my feet. 'Of course, there have been some upsetting episodes.'

'Celia's death? She was a lovely soul. Confused towards the end. But now she's one with the universe.'

'Did you know her well?' Kim asked.

'It was hard to know Celia. Violet was so good to her. A true friend. I know she went out that day to do some shopping, but no one can blame her for that. It's impossible to be a carer twenty-four-seven for someone. We all need our alone time.'

'Were you here the day Celia died?' I asked. 'Were you here on the estate?'

She hesitated. 'No,' she said. 'I had a doctor's appointment in town.'

It didn't seem right to pry. 'And of course,' I continued, 'there was Joe Porter.'

Naya shuddered. 'He was a horrible man,' she said. 'Quite disturbed.'

'Mentally, do you mean?'

'One evening, I had some friends over for dinner. We had a party. Quite a large party.' Naya smirked. 'It meant many cars were parked outside and on the road through the estate. I was on my morning walk the next day when Joe Porter came racing up to me. He was furious.'

'About what?'

'One of my friends had parked slightly across his driveway. Joe could still get his car out, but he had to go around. Well, the way he carried on, you'd think we'd driven through his house. I lowered his energies somewhat through a channelling process and thought that was the end of it.'

Kim spoke up. 'And it wasn't?'

'A few days later, Ramona went out to her car and found it had been keyed. Someone had marked all along one side.'

'And you're sure it was Joe?' I said.

There was movement in the doorway, and Ramona Coxon appeared. She gave us a shy smile as Naya turned to her. 'I've been filling them in on Joe.'

'Oh,' Ramona said. 'That nasty man.'

'See. Even Ramona disliked him, and she never bad-mouths anyone.'

'He damaged my car,' Ramona said glumly.

'I chipped in to have it repaired,' Naya added. 'These days, she parks in the driveway.'

'You're from Melbourne?' I asked.

'Mordialloc,' Ramona replied.

I nodded. 'It's lovely being near the water.'

'I love the sea.'

Kim spoke. 'How long have you been here?'

'About six months. I'll be heading back to Melbourne soon. My mother's not well.'

Naya turned to us. 'Although,' she said, 'Ramona's got a boyfriend. Someone she's been seeing. I haven't met him yet, though he's *quite* handsome.'

'A girl's got to have *some* secrets,' Ramona said, smiling.

'Show them the picture,' Naya urged, turning to us. 'The one you took last month.'

Reluctantly, Ramona brought up a picture on her phone. It showed her standing beside a handsome young man with a flowering jacaranda in the background.

'Goodness,' Kim said. 'He's *nice*. Does he have a brother?'

Ramona smiled. 'I'm afraid not.'

'You're not stealing him away from Cape Carson, are you?' I asked.

'Maybe.' Ramona turned to Naya. 'I better get moving. I've transcribed those chapters when you're ready.'

'Wonderful. Leave them in my office, and I'll see to them

shortly.'

'I'll go out and pick up that printing.'

'Fantastic.'

As Ramona disappeared down a hallway, Naya turned to us. 'Ramona's wonderful,' she said in a low voice. 'I hope she never leaves. She does everything: all my marketing, administration, even the shopping.'

'Good people are hard to find,' I agreed.

'She just cut her hair, though. It was to keep her boyfriend happy, although I think it looked better before.' She turned to Kim. 'By the way, I've got another book coming out soon.'

Kim smiled. 'Wonderful,' she said. 'We love supporting local authors.'

I knew that was true. Libraries always supported authors in their area. Although, I couldn't help but wonder what Kim thought of Naya and her books. We thanked the woman for her time and said goodbye.

Ramona was leaving the house just as we reached our jeep. She cast a furtive glance in our direction. *She wants to tell us something.* Naya was inside, so it seemed safe to talk. We headed over to where the girl was lingering beside her car.

'I heard you talking to Naya about Joe Porter,' she said.

'It seems he wasn't the most liked person on the estate,' I said.

'I think there's something you should know,' Ramona said,

glancing back towards the house. 'Naya and Joe had a huge argument after my car got damaged. One evening, she saw him in the park and demanded he reimburse me for damages.'

'What did Joe say?' Kim asked.

'He laughed in her face. Said he wasn't paying her a cent. Then Naya said something that surprised me.' Ramona glanced about fearfully as she lowered her voice. 'Naya said the sooner that Joe was dead, the better.'

Kim and I thanked her for the information and returned to my jeep. Minutes later, we were heading back to town.

'So much for enlightenment,' Kim said.

'It sounds like everyone had issues with Joe.'

'We haven't spoken to Luca yet.' I glanced at my watch. 'But he'll have to wait. I've got something on tonight.'

'Oh?' Kim grinned. 'A big date?'

'No,' I said, sighing. 'I'm heading to Dinosaur Town.'

16

'Now,' Jim Turner said, 'you're probably wondering why we're dressed like this.'

'The thought had crossed my mind,' I admitted.

I was sitting at Jim Turner's dining room table. That alone was something I never thought I'd experience. While Jim had always struck me as a pleasant guy, I'd never thought there'd be a time when I'd be in his home.

What made this even more bizarre were the outfits he and the others around the table were wearing. Everyone was in either brown leather or black fabric, all trimmed in bronze. Jim was dressed like a circus ringmaster. His top hat was decorated with tiny glittering cogs and gears. Samantha, sitting beside him, was a cancan girl. She wore black fingerless gloves and a corset adorned with bronze keys. The other two players of the game—Beth and Jeremy Twill—looked like a 1920's aviator and pirate respectively. Jeremy was an engineer who worked for the council. His daughter, Beth, was in her final year at Cape

Carson High.

'It's steampunk,' Beth explained. 'A subculture that creates an alternative history world that mashes together Victorian society with retro steam technology and air ships.'

Okay, I thought. This was making a little more sense. I had heard something about steampunk. It had started with books and branched into comics, music, art and clothing. There were even conventions held where everyone turned up in costume.

'Cosplay isn't compulsory,' Jim added, 'although it is fun. Samantha's a member of the Cape Carson Frocked Up group. They help us make our outfits.' Jim leaned close. 'If you join, Rosie, you can have an outfit too.'

As much as I admired their clothing—the styling was truly excellent—I was pretty sure this would be my one and only visit to Dinosaur Land. Before I could verbalise this, however, Jim turned to Jeremy.

'And Trixie too,' Samantha said. 'I'm sure we could get something custom-made for her.'

Trixie lay down and hid her head under her front paws.

Jim turned to Jeremy. 'Hang on,' he said. 'Rosie hasn't even seen the game in action. Would you like to explain Jurassic Lord?'

Jurassic Lord—AKA Jeremy Twill—nodded.

He was English and tall and balding man with a caramel-coloured, hook moustache and a jovial twinkle in his eye. 'Welcome, visitor,' he said. 'A Steamcar in Dinosaur Town is a roleplaying game where we struggle to reach the Time portal on the other side of the game while remaining ahead of our pursuers.'

'Okay,' I said. 'And they are?'

'They come from several kingdoms, although I'll just give you the main ones: Tyrannosaurus Rex Mesa, the Valley of Brontosaurus, the Island Kingdom of Triceratops, and Pterodactyl Cove.'

At the mention of this last one, the game players gave a collective shudder. 'What's wrong with Pterodactyl Cove?' I asked.

'Just don't go there,' Samantha advised.

'Okay,' I said, mystified. 'I'll do my best not to.'

'We had another player—Jason—known to us as Steam Warrior who got caught in a Transportation Vortex,' Beth said. 'Landed there, and didn't make it out alive. It was...not a good ending.'

Jeremy continued. 'Players get talent cards that dictate their abilities,' he said. 'And each person rolls the dice to see what actions they should take.' He pointed to the side of the board. 'You're starting here. You need to roll anything from three to sixty-one.'

'But just don't roll twenty-nine,' Beth said.

The others laughed.

'Yes,' Jim agreed. 'Don't roll twenty-nine.'

'What happens if I roll twenty-nine?'

'You don't want to know.'

Actually, I did want to know, but I thought it was best to keep moving.

'Anyway,' Jeremy continued. 'Roll any other number, and you can use that nearby transportation hub to move over here.' He pointed to a spot in the middle of the board where the other player's tokens were assembled. 'You can join us as we confront Steamasaurus.'

'Steamasaurus?' I said.

'Part dinosaur,' Samantha said. 'Part steam engine.'

Beth added. 'The morphing of steam parts to his reptilian body sent him insane.'

'I imagine it would,' I said. 'I'd go insane if that happened to me.'

Jeremy dealt me game cards that gave me my abilities. It turned out I was high on communication and agility but low on strength and luck.

'Think of yourself as a diplomat,' Beth advised. 'An agile diplomat.'

An agile diplomat, I thought. *I can live with that.*

As I was the newest player, I had to go first. Jeremy handed me five dice with a dizzying array of numbers on them. They bore no resemblance to any set of dice I'd ever used before.

'Oh!' Jim said. 'I just remembered. Rosie hasn't got a name yet.'

'Um, it's Rosie,' I said.

'No, no,' Samantha protested. 'You need an appropriate name for Dinosaur Town.'

Beth pondered. 'How about...wait! What about Rachet Rosie!'

'That's fantastic!' Jeremy agreed. '*Rachet*!'

I thought Rosie was a good name, although I thought I could survive the evening as Rachet.

'Okay,' Jeremy said. 'Roll the dice, Rachet.'

Everyone wished me good luck, and I rolled the dice. They scattered across the board, knocking over one of the other player tokens. No one seemed too worried, however, as they counted the total.

'So that's seventeen,' Jeremy said. 'Twenty-one...and eight makes...' His voice trailed away.

'Oh dear,' Samantha said. 'That's twenty-nine.'

An ominous silence settled over the table.

'Maybe Rachet can roll again,' Beth suggested.

The others gravely shook their heads. 'No,' Jim said. 'That would be cheating.'

'What's happening?' I asked, mystified.

Jim pointed. 'Twenty-nine automatically puts you in the doorway of the Transportation Hub to Pterodactyl Cove,' he said.

'Oh,' I said. 'Well, it is someone else's turn now?'

'Not yet,' Beth said. 'Your power dice rolled a thirteen, which means you go again.'

Lucky me.

I rolled, and the group grimly added up my total.

'My goodness,' Samantha said. 'That's unfortunate.'

Jeremy picked up a scenario card and read it out. 'You've entered Pterodactyl Cove,' he said. 'You've arrived at a time when...' His voice trailed off as he sadly shook his head. 'Well, that's bad luck. The pterodactyls have returned from their hunt empty-handed, or empty-clawed, as the case may be.' His eyes met mine. 'Rachet. You must use your agile diplomatic skills to talk your way out of this.'

'Talk?' I said. 'To the dinosaurs?'

'They're intelligent,' Samantha said. 'Although not known for their chattiness. You have to stand your grand, but not be condescending.'

'And don't mention asteroids,' Jim added. 'They're a bit touchy about them.'

I hadn't intended bringing asteroids into the conversation, though I appreciated the advice.

'Well, um, mighty pterodactyl people,' I stammered. 'It's awfully nice to meet you. I'm Rosie...I mean, Rachet, and I'm hoping my accidental arrival here can herald a new era of peace.' I faltered. 'That's about it.'

Jeremy rolled a dice. 'Oh dear,' he said. 'Typhys, Lord of the Pterodactyls, has just bitten off one of your legs.'

'*He's bitten off my leg?* I thought I was an agile diplomat!'

'Not agile enough,' Samantha informed me sadly.

'Roll again, Rachet,' Jim said. 'If you roll under twenty, you can escape using a Steampower card.'

I rolled the five dice. 'Hmm,' I said. 'Fifty-four. That's a little higher than twenty.'

'Try using your diplomacy again,' Samantha advised.

'Oh Typhys,' I began. 'I know we got off on the wrong foot...I mean...anyway...but peace is still possible—'

Jeremy rolled a dice, and I lost my other leg.

'Rachet's in trouble,' Beth said, delivering what had to be the biggest understatement of the century. She turned to the others. 'We should launch a rescue mission.'

This suggestion was met with silence.

'No,' Jim said, finally. 'I'll be right. I'll just hang here for a while.'

'Me too,' Samantha said. 'I'd like to help, but my strength's a little low. It's at...er, ninety-three.'

Jurassic Lord rolled a few more times, and I responded with my own dice throws. It would have made more sense if I'd been called Kamakazi Rosie, as I quickly lost both arms.

I sat back, feeling oddly disappointed. I'd played most of the well-known board games: Monopoly, The Game of Life, Clue. I'd even played chess drunk once and beaten Kim, who was an excellent player but had consumed six piña coladas on an empty stomach. Still, this was the worst gaming defeat of my life.

'So I'm dead,' I said, staring at the board.

'Not quite,' Jim said.

'But...but...my arms and legs have been ripped off by a dinosaur.'

'You're injured,' Jeremy informed me. 'But still alive.'

'And you still have another roll,' Beth pointed out in an effort to be optimistic. 'And let's not forget your high level of agility.'

My agility hadn't helped me much so far. Regardless, I rolled again. The sound of the dice landing on the gameboard was met with rapturous applause.

'The hub's reopened!' Jim yelled. 'Quickly, Rachet! Get to the gateway!'

'But her speed is limited because of her injuries!' Samantha cried.

'She can still roll!'

'The dice?' I said, confused.

'No!' Jim urged. 'Your body! Your body!'

'You gain an extra dice by physically doing the action!' Beth yelled.

I quickly discovered that you can't roll and sit in a chair at the same time. Within seconds, I was on the floor, rolling about on the rug like a leper with St Vitus Dance. By now I was operating on a purely competitive level and didn't care how I looked. I *liked* board games. I *won* them all the time. In our household, I'd triumphed in Monopoly so often that everyone refused to play me. Once, Nan and Amanda even insisted on checking my sleeves for hundred dollar bills.

'Roll Rachet! Roll!' Samantha yelled.

It quickly became a chant as everyone joined in.

'Roll Rachet! Roll! Roll Rachet! Roll! Roll Rachet! Roll!'

After what seemed an eternity, I heard dice being thrown again. 'Oh, Rachet,' Jeremy said sadly. 'Typhys has caught you.'

I peered up at them, dizzy and sweating, my hair a shambles and my clothing in disarray. Trixie gave a worried whine.

'Oh dear,' I said. 'What happens now?'

'It's bad,' Jeremy continued. 'You've been decapitated and disembowelled—and not in that order.'

'Well.' I struggled to my feet, feeling more disappointed than I'd expected. Never had I been defeated so quickly in a board game. 'That's bad luck, but I know now: never roll twenty-nine.'

The others continued the game for the next hour. Watching them working together as they struggled across the fantasy landscape seemed like quite a fun experience. I almost felt sad that I'd been knocked out so quickly. At the end of the evening, I snapped a few photos and wished everyone goodnight.

Samantha and Jim saw me to the front door. She slid her arm around Jim's waist as I said goodbye.

'Oh,' I said. 'That's a nice surprise. You two are dating?'

'We sure are,' Samantha said. 'We have so many interests in common.'

The door shut, and the cool evening closed around me. I turned to Trixie. 'Well,' I said. 'Jim Turner and Samantha Greco. I'm glad someone's a winner.'

17

'Ah!' Luca Romero said, throwing his arms into the air. 'Bella!'

'Hello, Luca,' I said. 'Do you remember us?'

Kim, Trixie, and I were on Luca's front doorstep. It was the following day and we still had one resident to interview: the womanising gigolo that every woman with an ounce of common sense avoided like the plague. Luca was wearing his trademark white suit; I wondered if he ever wore anything else.

'Remember you?' he said. 'I never forget beautiful women!'

Trixie yowled.

I know how you feel!

'Do you mind if we have a chat?' I asked.

He waved us into his home. At least one thing I could say in his favour. Luca kept a clean house. Spotless, as a matter of fact. It was like walking into a showroom. The décor was Spanish: from the imported furniture to the wall hangings of Ibiza. Luca seemed to adore an artist named Alejos Lorenzo.

'These are wonderful,' I said and meant it. 'Very colourful.'

'There are so many beautiful things in this world,' Luca said, grabbing some water and glasses. 'They must be celebrated.'

We went out onto his back deck, where we sat around a red, orange, and green tiled coffee table. Luca gave us a brief bio of his life: he'd worked as a chef for most of his career before moving to Melbourne. He'd been married for a few years before his wife left for London—without him—and he relocated to Cape Carson. Luca had lived in Sandcastle Village for six years and had loved every moment of it.

'You've had quite an international life,' Kim said. 'You must find it quiet here.'

'Quiet is good,' Luca said. 'All I am missing is a beautiful woman to share my life.'

His eyes flickered between us as if trying to decide which was a better catch. 'Well,' I said, keen to keep us focused. 'I'm sure that will happen eventually. At least your neighbours seem lovely.'

'Wonderful people.'

'And so sad that Celia passed away.'

'A lovely woman struck down by a cruel illness. It was a blessing in the end.'

'And Joe Porter only died a month ago.'

Luca hesitated. 'Another tragedy,' he said. 'These things happen.'

I gave a hollow laugh. 'You're the only person to describe it as a tragedy,' I said. 'Everyone else said Joe was a terrible man.'

'I don't like to say bad things, but he certainly knew how to—how shall I say it—ruffle the feathers?'

I nodded, waiting.

'You will have noticed our magnificent park,' Luca continued. 'Many residents use it each day. It is relaxing. We enjoy nature. I usually take a walk late after the day's heat has passed. Joe Porter also would take walks at this time.

'Often, I would observe him dropping rubbish as he walked. At first, I ignored it, but my patience wore thin as time went on. One day I confronted him. I said, *Joe, I see once more that you are dropping rubbish onto the ground*. And you know what he says? He says *So what? What business is it of yours?*

'I tried to be polite, but there was no way to discuss it—how do you say—amicably. He raised his voice and laughed at me. He called me names that were racist. I lifted my hand to strike him, and he said I would be sued. Joe said he had much money and he would crush me. I did nothing, much to my regret.'

'What happened then?'

'A few days later, I went for my morning walk. That's when I realised my letterbox was gone.'

'Gone?'

'I had a large, stone letterbox. A strong letterbox that cost me many dollars. It was taken. Ripped from the ground.'

'And you believe Joe stole it?'

Luca shrugged. 'Who else would do such a thing?' He leaned forward. 'This was only a few weeks before Joe died. You know what I think? God almighty struck him down.' An unsettling smile played on his lips. 'They say God works in mysterious ways. Some ways are not so mysterious!'

The man laughed openly. We joined in, although our own laughter was rather less raucous. 'The day that Celia died,' I continued, 'someone was seen going to her door. Do you know anything about that?'

'A person at her door? You mean one of her sons?'

'No. It was someone else. It could have been a gardener.'

Luca pursed his lips. 'A gardener?' he said. 'I do not think so. They are here on Mondays? Are they not?'

'Never any other day?' Kim asked.

'No, I—wait. Yes, I have seen them here at other times.'

'Really?' I said. 'No one else mentioned that.'

'It's when a tree has a broken branch or a tree is diseased. They cut it down because it is dangerous. A tree in the back of Olivia and Henry's yard fell over in a storm. It only just missed their back porch. Since then, the gardeners have been more careful.' He thought before raising in index finger to the air. 'Wait! I did see a gardener here on Sunday!'

'Are you sure?' Kim asked.

'Yes. I did not think about it till now, but it was when I was returning from my shopping. You saw my car in the driveway?

The 1966 Thunderbird?'

I had noticed it. The car was hard *not* to notice. The sapphire blue Ford Thunderbird was stunning. It was parked at a jaunty angle in the driveway as if daring people to notice it.

'It's lovely,' I said.

'I had pulled into my driveway when I saw a gardener in the park.'

'Working in the park?'

'It is hard to say. You catch glimpses of people through the trees. I saw one of the gardeners.'

'It was definitely a gardener? It couldn't have been another maintenance person?'

He shook his head. 'The uniform was the same. The same colour. Even the logo on the back.'

'And what time was this?'

'Around lunch. I always come home to see the midday news.'

Nodding thoughtfully, I thanked Luca for his time, and we got up to leave.

'But it seems all we have talked about is death and strange visitors,' he said. 'I must show you around my home.'

He insisted on giving us the whole tour. The more I saw, the more I wondered if he could be some kind of cleanness freak. To my way of thinking, the cleaner the house, the stranger the owner!

The last room was the master bedroom. He paused outside the door, gripping the handle before turning to us. 'You will *love* this room,' he murmured, winking. 'It is my favourite.'

Luca flung the door open, and Kim and I leaned in. The interior was dimly lit, with filtered light streaming in through chiffon curtains.

Two doors led off: one to a marble-clad ensuite, the other to a vast walk-in wardrobe. The only furniture in the bedroom was the bed. I'd seen queen and king-sized beds, but I'd never seen a bed this size before. It took up so much room that two people couldn't have squeezed past it. One would have to crawl across—which was probably how Luca liked it.

A single painted fresco of three figures dominated two of the walls. The image on the far left was of a ruggedly built man with sweptback black hair and an improbably dainty moustache. Bare-chested, he was thrusting his arm out like a Russian Cossack dancer.

Although the man bore an unerring resemblance to Luca, the body was so large that his head looked impossibly tiny.

What hovered before the painted man was an enormous cupid shooting an arrow. Every cupid I'd ever seen was of a small baby or child. This cupid was enormous and also bore an odd resemblance to Luca, albeit minus the moustache. My eyes moved to the arrow's victim, a Grecian maiden with only diaphanous scraps of fabric to cover her lady parts. One hand was flung protectively across the chest. The other was thrown back across her forehead as if she were about to faint.

I didn't blame her. If Pin-head or giant Cupid were heading in my direction, I'd faint too. Oddly, however, her expression was either lecherous, hopeful, or drug-addled. Maybe all three. It was hard to tell.

To make matters worse, a disco ball hung from the ceiling. It had begun to turn the moment the door had been flung open. Now, tiny dots of light cruised slowly around the room. Worse still, the ceiling above was sheathed in mirrors reflecting everything below.

Until now, little of my focus had been on the bed. As my eyes grew accustomed to the faint light, I saw the bedspread portrayed the faces of a man and woman, their lips only inches from each other. It had to be custom designed; the man's face looked remarkably like Luca's. Even the moustache was his. The woman's identity was impossible to determine.

At least the artist had succeeded here: the woman's wide-eyed expression was either shock or horror. Possibly she represented all women when confronted with the Lucas of the world.

Our host said nothing, and neither did we. Trixie tilted her head in either confusion or amazement.

'Goodness,' Kim finally said.

'Yes,' I said. 'Goodness.' I glanced at my watch. 'Well, we'd better get going. We've got that...er, meeting.'

'Oh yes,' Kim agreed, peering at her wrist despite not wearing a watch. 'Look at the time. We'd better go.'

We started for the front door with Luca in close pursuit. 'You ladies must return,' he gushed. 'I always have a bottle of *Finca Allende Aurus* at hand.'

'Oh yes,' I said, thinking I'd bring a shield and a sword if I ever returned. 'I'll keep that in mind.'

18

Kim and I didn't speak again until we were almost back at Percy Street.

'Well,' I said, finally. 'If you're ever stuck for a date—'

'Don't even joke about it.'

'Okay.' I stifled a grin. 'That was quite a disco ball. I haven't seen one like that since *Saturday Night Fever*.'

Kim groaned. 'I'll never watch that movie the same way again.'

Pulling onto Percy Street, I pointed to Sandy's Diner. 'Hey,' I said. 'There's my favourite grandmother.'

Nan was out the front of Sandy's with her gang, yarnbombing one of the local street signs.

'Excellent,' Kim said. 'Let's stop here. I need coffee and food.' She paused. 'Maybe even scotch to drive the sight of Luca's bedroom from my mind.'

I pulled over, and we piled from the car. Trixie barked and went racing up to Nan.

'Heavens!' Nan said. 'There's my favourite beagle.'

'Followed by your favourite granddaughter,' I added. 'Feel like joining us for a spot of lunch?'

'Sure do. All this textile terrorism wears out an old girl like me.' Nan left Irene, and Thelma and the others to continue while she took a break.

We left Trixie outside with a water bowl before heading into Sandy's. The place was pumping with the music of Elvis in the background. Most booths were taken, but one became vacant just as we arrived.

'How's your investigation into Celia's death progressing?' Nan asked.

'We're getting there,' I said.

We related what we'd discovered so far, including a description of Luca's love pad. Nan slapped her knee as she hooted with laughter.

'He's a legend in his own mind,' she chuckled.

'Luca particularly liked Kim,' I teased, turning to her. 'I can give him your number if you like.'

'Don't you dare!'

Nan stroked her chin. 'But Luca may have been helpful,' she said. 'He was certain her killer was dressed as a gardener?'

'So he said,' I replied.

'Then it's worthwhile visiting the gardening company. Check out their staff.'

'You know, that's a good idea. We've assumed the person only *looked* like a gardener until now. If the killer actually wore a company uniform, he might work for them.'

'It could be case-closed,' Kim said. 'Unless the killer stole one of their uniforms.'

I agreed that was a possibility. We finished our meal and headed out to the street. By now, the other ladies had finished fully yarnbombing the sign.

It was a sight to behold, with alternating rows of rainbow colours running from top to bottom.

'It's not subtle,' I said.

'Life's too short to be subtle,' Nan advised.

Kim, Trixie, and I returned to the car where I rang Doris and gave her an update on what we'd learned. I told her we still had a few leads to follow up.

'Well,' Doris said, 'be careful. The killer may have killed twice before, and he—or she—probably won't hesitate to kill two women and a small dog. Even a cute beagle like Trixie.'

After promising we'd be careful, we got the name of the gardening company from her. Ten minutes later, we pulled up in front of Dell's Garden Centre. Graham was a kindly man with a broad, friendly face and brown eyes and hair. He had just sold a woman half a dozen proteas when we arrived.

'Rosie Ryan!' he said. 'Did your grandmother send you out for another rose bush?'

'We've already got enough to sink a ship. Now, I understand you also offer gardening services.'

Graham nodded. 'It's a sideline we started about a year back,' he explained. 'Took a while to get going, but these days it's almost as busy as the centre.'

I told him we were trying to work out if a member of their staff had visited Sandcastle Village the day of Celia's death. Graham quickly checked his computer.

'No,' he said. 'We only go there every third Monday. We're not due again till next week. Unless there's an emergency like a fallen tree. And then someone calls us.'

'And your staff?' I said. 'Have you had them long?'

'Ages. The ones who go onsite have worked at the centre for years.'

'You haven't had any uniforms stolen?' Kim asked.

Graham frowned. 'Funny you should mention that. One of the guys said something about some missing overalls.'

'Is there any way of seeing who could have taken them?' I asked. 'Do you have cameras?'

'Yep. I haven't bothered checking them, though, because I wasn't sure—and it's only a uniform anyway.'

'Can we take a look?'

Graham laughed. 'I think that can be arranged,' he said. 'It won't be exciting viewing, though. The camera just faces the door, and you see the same people go in and out all day.'

He set us up in front of a monitor in his back office, and we started playing the files. Graham wasn't kidding about the excitement level.

After he pointed out the half a dozen employees authorised to go into that section, we saw the same people going in and out all day.

'Whoever said investigating was exciting?' Kim asked.

'Certainly not me,' I said.

Fortunately, the camera was motion detected, so we weren't forced to watch every single minute of the last few weeks. However, it still took time as we trawled through them. Trixie eventually fell asleep, and I was almost the same until Kim cried out and pointed.

'Look!' she said. 'There!'

We paused the playback and examined the footage. Kim was right. The guy wasn't an employee at the garden centre, and he hadn't appeared in any other footage. He had a rugged face, as if he'd been in a lot of fights, and a messy head of hair. Playing the footage back several times, it was clear he was going into the storeroom and leaving with a folded-up bundle.

'That's got to be a uniform,' I said.

'Absolutely,' Kim agreed. 'And guess what—I know that guy.'

'Who is it?'

'I don't know his name, but I've seen him at Penny's Pizza

Place on Second Avenue.'

'Isn't that just up the road from the library?'

'The call of the pizza is strong,' Kim informed me, 'especially when we're weeding out old stock from the library. And Penny sells pizza by the slice.'

'I can't argue with that. Is he a customer?'

'No. I've seen him working in the kitchen.'

We printed an image of the man to take with us, thanked Graham, and returned to my jeep. Driving through town, I wondered how this guy fitted into the mystery.

'It doesn't make sense,' Kim agreed. 'Why would a pizza cook suddenly decide to murder an old lady?'

'Maybe he was hired to kill her.'

Kim beamed. 'A pizza guy turned assassin!' she said. 'That's so mafia!'

'Do you have to look pleased about it?'

'I can't help it! I love gangster movies: The Godfather, Goodfellas, Donnie Brasco.' She paused. 'Hang on. What if Penny's Pizza Place is a front? What if Penny is actually the local Godfather—no, *Godmother*—and she runs a string of assassins from the kitchen?'

'And what if you're an alien from Pluto?' I asked. 'Seriously, Kim! Penny's a sixty-five-year-old woman who sings in the choir at Saint Michael's on Sunday! She's not a mafia boss!'

Kim looked disappointed. 'We can't be certain.'

'If she's in disguise, it's the best disguise in history.'

Kim grumbled. 'It's your fault if we end up buried in concrete.'

'Sometimes I'd prefer it!' I grumbled back.

Somehow, we reached Penny's Pizza Place without killing each other.

The business had once been a service station. Bad times and another better-positioned servo down the road had left it empty and the owner bankrupt. It had sat disused for the last few years until Penny had come along and turned it into a pizza place. The counter aimed directly onto the outdoor area where people sat around eating pizza on cheap, stainless steel chairs. The vast, old service station awning provided cover for customers. What had been the shop was now filled with ovens and benchtops.

I'd been to Penny's a few times.

Style wasn't a consideration. Fortunately, this was made up for by the quality of the product. It was quiet at this time of day, with only a handful of people sitting around. I vaguely recognized the young guy on the counter from a story I'd done about the Surf Lifesaving Club. I asked if we could see Penny, and we were soon grouped around the front counter.

'Do I know this guy?' Penny asked. She pushed back her greying, curly hair while peering short-sightedly at the image. 'Sure. It's Felix.'

'Felix?' I said.

'Felix Kent. He does the weeknights.'

'So he's not around now?' Kim asked.

'Not until six o'clock.' Penny lowered her voice. 'Is he in some kind of trouble?'

'Maybe,' I said quietly. 'Has he been in trouble before?'

Penny sighed. 'I don't want to talk out of turn, but Felix has had a rough life,' she said. 'Been in and out of jail since he was a kid. Mind you, I knew that when I hired him. He came here as part of a program to help rehabilitate offenders back into society. I've never had a problem with him. And he seems to have turned his life around. He's got a girlfriend and reckons he's saving to buy a house.'

'Is it possible to get his address?'

Penny pulled a face. 'I don't know about that,' she said doubtfully. 'I don't want to get involved. And besides, he hasn't actually done anything.'

'Just a general idea where he lives?' Kim prompted.

Penny hesitated. 'Melhouse,' she said. 'I can't say more.'

Melhouse was a small town northwest of Cape Carson. It wouldn't take us long to track him down. I glanced up at the menu. The smell of freshly cooked pizza bread and cheese was intoxicating.

'What do you recommend?' I asked.

'Ham and pineapple is popular.'

'*What?*'

Kim looked similarly shocked. 'It can't be,' she said.

'Seriously?' Penny said. 'You don't like ham and pineapple pizza?'

The debate about ham and pineapple pizzas had been going on in Australia for years.

While some people declared pineapple on a pizza to be a necessity, sensible people—like Kim and me—recognised pineapple on pizza for what it was: an unnatural crime against humanity.

However, I had to be diplomatic. 'Penny,' I said. 'It takes all kinds to make a world.'

I ordered Margherita while Kim got a few slices of Meat Lovers.

A few minutes later, we were back in the car with Trixie, eating pizza on the way to Melhouse.

'Ham and pineapple pizza,' I said and shuddered.

Kim shook her head sadly. 'Some people have no standards.'

19

We followed Donovan Street out of town and were driving through open countryside.

The pizza was soon finished, leaving us to watch the passing landscape. The weather was cool, but the sky was a single sheet of baby blue. Beneath it lay rolling hills. A mob of kangaroos went bounding out of sight. Cows chewed their cuds.

A solitary tractor driver, trundling down the road, gave us a country wave, and I waved back.

Trixie, in the back seat, stuck her head out of the window, and her ears flapped about wildly. Kim and I laughed at the sight, and Trixie gave some happy barks.

It didn't take long to reach Melhouse. The place was a tired little town surrounded by open fields. The main street had once been a strip of two dozen thriving businesses, but all that remained now were a service station, bakery, and general store. We pulled into the petrol station, where I filled up.

I went in to pay. 'You might be able to help,' I said to the attendant as I handed over my card. 'I'm going to Felix's place, but I've left his address at home. Do you know it?'

The guy behind the counter was chunky with a thick, black beard. 'Felix?' he said. 'Needs a haircut?'

'That's him.'

'Down the far end of Bryce Street.'

I thanked him and returned to the car. We found Bryce Street and followed it for about a kilometre. Just as the tarred road gave way to dirt, we spotted a solitary two-storey house, huddled under gumtrees, on the left. I would have thought the place abandoned if not for the rundown Ford parked alongside.

The house had once been a family home. The gardens had been neat, the lawn trimmed and the hedge shaped. Now the garden was overgrown, the lawns were a jungle, and the hedge an unruly mess. The house wasn't in any better shape. The paint was peeling in a hundred places. One of the upstairs windows was broken with a piece of plywood nailed across. The porch sagged at one end.

The trees beside the house almost seemed to bury it in darkness. One butted up directly against the building.

Someone should remove that tree, I thought. *It'll take out the whole house one day.*

Playground equipment—a swing set and a slide— sat in the front yard, rusty and knee-deep in African feather grass. A trampoline in questionable condition lay on its side at the far end of the driveway.

'Looks homely,' Kim said.

'As homely as the house from Psycho.'

'Let's hope that Felix Kent doesn't take after his mother.'

We cautiously approached the building. The only movement was a black and white pee wee bird. It gave a distinctive high-pitched cry before taking flight into nearby branches.

'Rosie,' Kim murmured as we approached. 'Have you thought about what we're going to say to this guy?'

'Not exactly. I'm making this up as I go.'

The front screen door was dusty. It was shut, though, and the door behind it open. I peered through to the interior. All I could make out was an old hall rug and gloom beyond.

'Hello?' I called.

My voice echoed down the dark hallway. There was not one scintilla of sound; time could have come to a standstill. I turned to Kim.

'I'm going in,' I said.

'Um. Isn't this breaking and entering *again*?'

It was impossible to miss her emphasis on that last word. Kim had issues with me entering people's homes without their permission.

She saw it as *breaking in,* whereas I saw it as *investigating*.

'Okay, Miss Goody Two-Shoes,' I said. 'I'll go around back

first to see if he's there.'

'And then?'

'If he's not, I'm going inside. Maybe he's had a medical episode.'

Kim folded her arms. 'Rosie,' she said. 'That's what you said at Glenn's Salvage Yard, and look what happened. The man attacked us with a pipe and tried to run us off the road.'

'Which was very inconsiderate considering I was checking on his wellbeing.'

Grumbling, Kim followed me as I rounded the house. I touched Felix's car. The bonnet was cold. He hadn't driven anywhere recently.

The backyard was a reflection of the front: messy and over-grown. Kudzu vine blanketed the trees out here and was slowly choking them to death. Peering into the undergrowth, I had the strange feeling that we were being watched. I stared into the mash of trees, vines, weeds, and grass. It was like staring into a mess of cotton at the bottom of a sewing basket.

I called out again.

Silence.

The back screen door was shut too, with the door behind it open, revealing an empty kitchen. I rapped hard on the door, yelled out and still got no answer.

I turned to Kim. 'You can't say I didn't try.'

Kim grimaced. Even Trixie gave a worried whine as I entered.

The interior smelt of beer, fried food, and neglect. No one was home, although I had no idea where Felix could have gone. Maybe he went for a walk. People did that.

Goodness, even *I* did it.

We searched from room to room; they were either empty or sparsely furnished. Maybe the few pieces of furniture the house contained had come with the place. Although Penny had said Felix had turned over a new leaf, there was no evidence of it here. Everything reeked of an out-of-control life.

Reaching the bottom of the stairs, I called again, and the only answer was the faint echo of my own voice. We clattered up to a single hallway where rooms led off both sides. We glanced into each. Most were empty again, although I spied a pile of clothing in one.

'Hello?' I said.

Pushing the door open, I saw a pair of jeans on the floor, a t-shirt, a milk crate used as a table, and an unmade bed. I was half-expecting to see a man asleep on the bed, snoring like a baby. Instead, it was empty with no sign of the occupant.

'Nice to see a man who knows how to look after himself,' Kim muttered.

'A happy homemaker, he's not. What are those papers?'

Pages of an official document and some cash sat on the milk crate. Kim rounded the bed. 'This is a passport application,' she said. 'Maybe he was planning a holiday.'

Everyone's going on holidays, I thought. *Glenn had travel brochures too.*

I left Kim to examine the remaining paperwork, and continued down the hall. The bathroom was at the end, with the door half open and light streaming across the tiles. I called out *hello* again as I leaned into the room, but the word caught in my throat as I saw the man sprawled in the bath. He lay like a dead spider, with arms and legs askew, his mop of hair half across his face. A sharp-edged blade stuck out from the middle of his chest. He was shirtless, wearing only a pair of jeans and joggers.

'Rosie?' Kim called out. 'I found something interesting.'

There's something interesting here too I wanted to say, but the sight of the dead man had stolen my voice. Instead, I took a deep, shuddering breath to calm myself. I inhaled something sweet. What is that? Not a men's cologne. *Perfume.*

There was movement behind me, and I half-turned to see Kim. She peered past me.

'Oh dear,' she said, swallowing. 'He's dead?'

'I doubt he's taking a nap.'

Trixie whined. Leaning her head against me, I ruffled her neck.

'It's okay, girl,' I said.

She whined again and I inhaled.
What is that? Petrol?

Although disturbing the crime scene was a *no-no*, I had to make sure he really was dead. Carefully stepping to the edge of the bath, I reached down and took his pulse.

Yes. Definitely kaput. Getting stabbed in the heart does nothing for a person's longevity. His skin was warm; Felix Kent hadn't been dead long.

A bang came from downstairs. Kim's eyes met mine, and we fled the bathroom and started down the hallway. There was another bang, followed immediately by a *whoosh*, and a massive explosion of fire erupted up the stairwell.

Kim screamed. We edged to the top of the stairs and peered down. Whoever had set the fire had done a good job of it. The stench of petrol choked the air with the stairs already well alight. The flames trailed off into the other downstairs rooms too. An empty fuel can lay amidst the blaze.

'We can't get down there,' I said.

'Are there backstairs?' Kim asked.

'I don't think so.'

'I'll check.'

I got on the phone and rang 000. By the time I'd hung up, Kim had searched the other rooms and returned looking grim. 'There are no stairs,' she said. 'And the drop to the ground is twenty feet.'

Smoke was already billowing up the stairs in great clouds.

'How long do you think they'll be?' Kim asked.

'Too long. The nearest fire station is in Cape Carson.'

'I've got an idea,' Kim said, leading me back to the bedroom. She flung the window open and peered down. 'We can push the mattress out and use it to cushion our fall.'

'Do you really think we can fit that thing out the window?'

Kim frowned. 'Maybe not.'

It was more likely the fire brigade would find us here, trapped with a mattress jammed in the window. Not quite the death scene I had in mind. I'd always preferred something more peaceful. Like falling asleep in an aged care facility at the age of ninety-nine while watching an episode of *Murder, She Wrote*.

I could toss Trixie out the window. Although she'd probably survive the drop, it might be at the cost of a broken leg or two. 'That branch,' Kim said, pointing to a nearby tree. 'I can reach it.'

'What?' I peered at the branch. It was about five feet away and below us. 'Not unless you've got rubber arms.'

'I can jump.'

'It's too far.'

'I did gymnastics at school for three years before I started running. Came third in the state for my age. I can make it.' Kim scrambled out the window and perched on the sill like a bird ready to fly. 'Stay here.'

'Uh, sure. I was about to take a shower, but if you insist…'

Kim took a deep breath, then pushed hard with her legs and flung out her arms like a gymnast leaping for the horizontal bar at the Olympics. Time seemed to stand still—and then her hands grasped the branch, and she swung back and forth from it like a monkey. She dragged herself to the trunk and shimmied her way down to the ground.

'I'm okay!' she yelled.

Trixie barked.

'Good!' I called back. 'That makes one of us. If you have any idea how I can get down—'

But Kim had already disappeared around the side of the building. I coughed. Smoke was pouring up the stairs in great voluminous clouds. Something shattered downstairs. Racing to the door, I pushed it shut and jammed sheets across the bottom.

Trixie gave a worried whimper, and I dropped to one knee. 'It's okay, girl,' I said. 'The fire brigade will be here soon, and then...'

My voice trailed off.

Yes, I thought. *The fire brigade will be here soon, but maybe not soon enough.*

'Rosie!'

I returned to the window. Kim had dragged the trampoline around from the back of the house and positioned it below. It was still a big drop—and the trampoline was in questionable condition—but it was an improvement.

'Bless you, Kim!' I yelled.

I scooped Trixie into my arms, told her *it will be okay*, and gently dropped her to the waiting trampoline below.

She landed, bounced awkwardly once or twice, and Kim dragged her free.

Now it was my turn. I shakily climbed out the window, and sat my bottom on the sill.

All I had to do now was jump. Which was simple enough, except I couldn't actually release the window sill because my hands were gripping it like talons. To make matters worse, the distance between me and the trampoline seemed to have increased tenfold.

'What are you waiting for?' Kim yelled.

'Christmas!'

'Well,' she said. 'It's almost here. Jump!'

Something exploded from within the house, and the entire building shuddered. Bracing my feet against the wall, I took a deep breath and pushed off. It wasn't so much a leap as a flailing fall into the unknown—and it seemed to go on forever. I saw Trixie's head swivel in confusion, unable to work out why I'd thrown myself helplessly off the side of the building. Kim's jaw dropped as slow puzzlement filled her face.

From the deep recesses of my mind, a memory popped into my head of an unfortunate seagull that I'd once seen on Percy

Street. The poor thing had a broken wind and was missing one leg. It tried launching itself off the footpath several times, like an early Wright brothers plane. I had been in the process of going to its rescue when it gained momentum and flew across the street—straight into the path of the 5.15pm bus from Melbourne.

I hit the trampoline.

I'm alive, I thought with a kind of hysterical wonder. *I'm alive!*

And then I was airborne again.

I thought of that unfortunate seagull before a vast wall of Kudzu vine loomed before me, and I ploughed into it. An eternity passed. Then I became aware of Kim's voice. She was screaming. There was other screaming too. No. Wailing. The fire brigade was arriving.

The vine had blanketed an overgrown grevillea. Clawing aside broken branches, I staggered from the undergrowth like some kind of fearsome monster, my hair unruly, skin scratched, and clothing torn.

'Rosie,' Kim said, drawing near. 'Are you all right?'

I was about to deliver an ironic retort, but then another explosion erupted from the old house.

'Better than Felix Kent,' I said.

20

'Goodness,' Todd Parker said, shaking his head. 'Two break and enters in one week. That's a record—even for you.'

'I wasn't actually breaking and entering—'

'Come to think of it,' he continued, determined to milk the moment for all he could get. 'We have repeat offenders who don't break and enter that often. They're usually on a weekly cycle. Some are fortnightly. Others only monthly.'

I groaned. 'I hate you.'

We were standing on the road outside what had been Felix Kent's home, although there wasn't a lot remaining. Two fire engines had turned up to put out the blaze, with another from the Country Fire Authority, who had extinguished spot fires around the surrounding property. The family home that had stood here for decades had been reduced to a pile of smouldering rubble.

'I thought someone had suffered a medical episode—' I tried again.

'Someone has,' Todd said. 'You.'

Ambulance officers had checked our injuries. Kim, of course, was completely unharmed. She was so indestructible that she probably should have donned a cape and fought crime on the weekends. Trixie was fine too. As for me, I would have been fighting fit if not for my bounce into the undergrowth. My knee was sore, and I was sure to come out in a dozen bruises.

'But let's forget your death wish for a moment,' Todd said, growing serious. 'Let's talk about Felix Kent and what you found.'

Kim and I went through what we'd learned over the last few days. Todd listened, took notes, and examined the photo that we'd printed from the footage at the garden centre. He finally closed his notebook and slipped it away.

'So maybe this man visited Celia Spalt the day she died,' he said. 'This means we need to take a closer look at her death. Maybe she really was murdered.'

'You believe us?' Kim said.

'You normally treat us like a pair of interfering crackpots,' I added.

'You *are* a pair of interfering crackpots!' Todd said, then smiled. 'But this Felix Kent was murdered for a reason, and it may be linked to Celia's death. Felix has a long history of break and enters. Car theft. An assault with a weapon. It's possible he

186

got wind of Celia's antiques and decided to rob her. Maybe he tailgated someone into the estate. He went to her place, maybe without the intention of killing her, but things went wrong.'

This all seemed reasonable—except I didn't think he was right.

'Todd,' I said. 'That doesn't explain Celia telling everyone at the Storytelling Tent that she'd seen a murder. It's too much of a coincidence that she died the next day. Celia was silenced on purpose.'

Kim said, 'And Violet doesn't think anything was stolen. If Felix went to steal something, then he left empty-handed.'

'He could have panicked,' Todd said. 'Or maybe he did steal something, and Violet didn't notice. She's an old lady and could be mistaken.'

There were times I wanted to hit Todd over the head, and this was one of those times. He had many good qualities. He was kind, had a great sense of humour, and was extremely good-looking. He could also be a pain in the posterior. 'Okay,' I said. 'I give up. We'll just keep investigating until we track down the killer.'

'Rosie,' Todd said. 'Don't be like that.'

I could feel myself getting wound up and was ready for a full scale argument. Trixie, however, chose that moment to nudge my leg. I looked down at her.

You clever dog, I thought. *You know me better than I know myself.*

'Okay,' I said shortly. 'Come on, Kim. We've done all we can here.'

'True,' Todd said, now also irritated. 'A man is dead, and a house has been burnt to the ground. That's hard to top.'

Grumbling, I stalked off with Trixie and Kim in my wake. We reached my car and piled in. As I angrily started the engine, I turned to Kim. 'What is it with that guy?' I demanded.

'You two are probably too similar.'

'*What?*' I turned to her in amazement. 'I'm nothing like Todd! He's stubborn!'

'Er, like you?'

Now I felt like throwing Kim out of the jeep. 'Is there anything else I should know?' I asked through clenched teeth.

'You have a dead frog in your hair.'

'*What?*'

'I thought it was a leaf—'

Once I'd gotten out of the car and shaken everything, both alive and dead, from my person, I got back in and drove us back to Cape Carson. It was late in the day now, and I was exhausted, hungry, and hurting. I dropped Kim off at her place and drove home.

'Hey Nan,' I said as I limped inside.

She was sitting at the dining room table. 'What happened to you?' she said. 'You look like you've been hit by a truck.'

'Only a small one.'

I sat down and told her about my day while she made me a cup of tea. She sat it in front of me before leaning against the kitchen bench.

'That Todd,' I groaned, as I sipped the tea. 'He's the most stubborn person I've ever met.'

Nan laughed. 'Almost as stubborn as you?'

I stared at her in amazement. 'Kim said the same thing! What is wrong with you people?'

Now Nan was laughing hard. 'Drink your tea, Rosie,' she said. 'Sometimes we can't see the forest for the trees.'

Grumbling under my breath, I went to my bedroom and settled down on my bed. I sipped my tea as I peered out the window and watched the darkening sky. Clouds had come over during the afternoon. There was no chance of rain, though. Yawning, I closed my eyes. I was exhausted. If I rested for a moment...

The next thing I knew, I was blinking and still sitting upright in bed. I'd been asleep. It was just before five. *I was more tired than I realised.* Climbing out of bed, I took a few steps before noticing how beaten up I felt. Landing in that grevillea had knocked me about more than I'd thought.

A quick shower would help. I went to the bathroom, washed, and got redressed. Nan was watching TV in the living room.

'I'm taking Trixie for a walk,' I announced.

'The fresh air will do you the world of good. And I hope you're not too bashed up. I'm planning more pickups.'

'Great. Nothing I love more than picking up other people's unwanted stuff.'

'That's my girl.'

I headed out the door with Trixie and down the street to where it met the bush. We took the trail towards the ocean and, a few minutes later, emerged at Cut Rock Lookout. Despite my body feeling like I'd been through a mincer, I immediately felt better. The smell of the ocean was invigorating. The waves pounded against the coast, sending a swell crashing into the crevice. Spray erupted from the crack and was cast high into the air.

I peered out at the ocean. There was no sign of whales. *They've already turned in for the day.* I leaned against the railing. The sky had obligingly decided to soothe my battered nerves. Scattered cloud shone with the last light of day. It lay like crimped crimson and gold wool across the vast sky, from the darkening bush to the horizon across the southern ocean.

It was a breathtaking spectacle, and I wasn't the only one to appreciate it. Several other people had stopped to stare.

'Fancy meeting you here.'

I glanced around and saw the other most stubborn person in Cape Carson.

'Oh,' I said. 'Hello, Todd.'

He was taking his three-legged greyhound dog, Rocko, for a walk. Trixie happily went up to Rocko and smelled him. They settled down together.

As much as I wanted to feel annoyed with Todd, I couldn't muster the energy. Now out of his cop uniform, Todd wore an Adidas t-shirt, a light jacket, and jeans. He was simply too handsome and the evening too beautiful for me to feel anything but happy.

'Feeling better now?' he asked.

'Pretty good,' I said. 'For an interfering crackpot.'

I stared at him in the deepening light and saw his barely suppressed grin. I couldn't help it. I burst out laughing.

'You're an annoying man, Todd Parker,' I said.

'Thanks. It doesn't come easily.'

We leaned against the railing and watched the overhead show. Gold had ridged the clouds now, and I felt the urge to take a photo. It would be a waste, though. Pictures were never the same. And nothing could recreate this special moment: leaning against a railing in the early evening of a long day, watching the sky kaleidoscope from one colour to the next, listening to the surging power of the ocean.

'That's quite a sight,' I said.

'There's none better,' Todd agreed.

'Got anything on for this evening?'

'Yvonne's making dinner,' Todd said. 'She's quite a cook.'

'Great,' I said, evenly. Todd's personal life was his own and none of my business. 'Anything else? Maybe another night in Lilliput?'

Todd had revealed his secret passion to me a while back. A model train enthusiast, he spent much of his spare time reconfiguring a huge trainset he'd been working on for years. It was quite a sight.

'Good things take time,' he said. 'And don't forget—that's our secret.'

I shrugged. 'There are stranger hobbies. I went to Jim's gaming night.'

'Really? The steam car thing?'

I told him about it and how Jim and Samantha were now an item. 'Really?' he said. 'I could tell he was interested but never thought he'd get anywhere with her. He's too...big and dorky, and she's too...'

'Short and gothic?'

'Yeah.'

We laughed again.

It was nice being here with Todd. I felt relaxed as if I could be myself with him. Why we argued was a mystery. Maybe Nan and Kim were right. Maybe Todd and I were stubborn. Maybe we were too similar.

The first chill of night made me shiver. I had to keep moving.

Wishing Todd goodnight, I headed down the hill where the town was slowly coming to life. Lights were on at cafes and restaurants. The boats at the jetty gently swayed in the water. Stars were appearing in the deepening sky.

A vehicle came up the road. I wouldn't have noticed it, except the car was so distinctive, and I'd seen it recently. The 1966 sapphire blue Thunderbird was owned by Luca Romero. The Spaniard sat crouched behind the wheel.

Out for the night.

Following the coastal path towards the lighthouse, I heard frantic barking from up ahead. Oddly enough, I recognised that bark. So did Trixie. Her ears pricked up as a stout figure emerged from the gloom.

'Hannah,' I said, surprised.

Her pug, Princess, barked even louder. 'Goodness! Rosie!' Hannah said. 'I didn't expect to see you down here.'

I told her I walked this way a lot, and Hannah said she came this way when the weather was good. As she spoke, I found myself peering at Hannah's face in the gathering darkness. She wore a barely concealed smirk, like a cat that had swallowed the proverbial canary. I made an innocuous comment about the weather, and she chortled with ill-concealed joy.

What is going on?

'You seem in a good mood,' I commented.

'Really?' she said. 'Oh, I've been thinking about going on a holiday. Somewhere overseas. It's nice to get away.'

Everyone's planning holidays, I thought. *Glenn Spalt, Felix Kent and now Hannah Foyle.* I wanted to talk more, but the woman wished me goodnight and marched on into the dark.

Now, I thought. *That's weird.*

I continued along the coastal path to the lighthouse. It was evening now, and the colour had faded from the sky. The water was dark and still. Although the lighthouse no longer shone out to sea, the floodlights at its base cast huge sloping cones of illumination across the cylindrical surface.

A running figure appeared.

'Kim!' I said.

'Hey, you,' Kim said, drawing to a stop. 'I thought you were in recovery.'

'My mind wouldn't let me.'

'I'm just at the end of a five-kilometre run.'

'I would have done the same except for...well...you know...it involves running...'

Kim peered out at the ocean. 'Thinking about life?'

'I've been thinking about this case,' I admitted and told her about bumping into Hannah Foyle. 'Nothing seems to fit together.'

We settled onto a nearby seat, and I continued. 'This whole thing started with Celia Spalt announcing at the Storytelling Tent that she'd witnessed a murder,' I said. 'The killing that she'd witnessed must have been that of Joe Porter.'

'That seems likely as he died only a month ago.'

'Poor Celia couldn't verbalise what she'd seen. But the killer must have been in the tent and went into a panic. If anyone took her seriously, then it was game over. Other people might make the connection to Joe Porter's death and then launch an investigation.'

'That makes sense. Celia's sons benefitted from her death, but they both have alibis. So her death seems related to Joe Porter. The question is, who benefitted from Joe's death?'

'Only a niece who lives in Marble Bar thousands of kilometres away—and his neighbours who all hated him. And it's quite a list.'

'You're not wrong there,' she said. 'Any of them could have contracted Felix Kent to kill Celia.'

'And Joe, for that matter.'

'So who was paying Felix?'

I sighed, thinking back to the interviews. 'Trudi Kendrix complained about Joe leaving his rubbish on the footpath,' I said. 'As a result, she became the victim of a hate campaign. Her reputation was ruined, and she was eventually fired from her job.'

'Although she seems to have done well for herself anyway.'

'Still, she was maliciously maligned. Who knows what she thinks? His lies could have destroyed friendships. Maybe even ended a relationship with a loved one. And stuff hangs around online for years. It could still be damaging her.'

'Okay,' Kim said, nodding. 'Then there's Vincent and his demon child, Graham. Vincent argued with Joe about stealing his roses. Next thing, Vincent's garden has been poisoned.'

'Which all seems like a complete overreaction.'

'Joe Porter doesn't seem to have done anything by half measures. And Vincent may not have killed Joe, but his son Graham is odd. Maybe Graham killed Joe.'

'Graham is odd,' I agreed. 'Although Graham couldn't have paid off Felix. He's a kid, not the Godfather of crime.'

'Vincent may have realised that Graham murdered Joe. To protect Graham, Vincent could have paid off Felix.'

'That's true,' I said. 'So who else do we have?'

'Well, there's Luca. He challenged Joe over littering, and the men argued. Luca had his letterbox stolen and Joe made racist remarks. That could have produced some real hatred.'

'So Luca's a possibility, too.' I sighed. 'And the list goes on. Olivia and Henry Rudd argued with Joe about being a peeping Tom, and their cat vanished. Hannah argued with Joe about her dog, and he tried to poison it. Naya's friends parked across Joe's driveway, and Ramona's car was damaged.' I shook my head. 'This is crazy. Everyone argued with Joe Porter and had good reasons to hate him. Still, none had a *really* good motive for murder.'

'People can get pretty upset about their animals being hurt. Olivia clearly unwell. Losing her cat may have pushed her over the edge. And Hannah's quite attached to her dog.'

I told her about meeting Hannah on the path and the woman's plans to go on a holiday. 'She seemed really smug about it,' I said. 'Almost elated.'

'Then we need to revisit her.'

I agreed. There had been something decidedly odd about Hannah Foyle.

What did she know that we didn't?

21

'Good grief!' I said. 'What are you ladies doing down here?'

Nan laughed. 'Textile terrorism!' she said. 'It's the perfect way to begin the day!'

It was seven-thirty in the morning, and I'd been on an early morning walk through town when Trixie and I had come across the bombers. Nan and the other members of the Yarn Bombers Association were busily decorating the public seat in front of the cinema. The piece of fabric they were using must have taken days to make.

I'd noticed earlier that Nan wasn't around when I showered and dressed. That hadn't surprised me much. Although her morning yoga was usually via an online class, she sometimes attended Seaside Yoga, a studio on Percy Street. What I didn't expect was an early morning yarn bombing raid.

I peered more closely at the fabric. It was an image of an early morning sunrise, and it fit perfectly over the front of the seat. 'That's very pretty,' I said. 'I'm surprised that you've taken so much trouble—huh?'

Nan and the others had erupted into peals of laughter.

Thelma nodded with satisfaction. 'That's what we were hoping for,' she said. 'It looks lovely—from the footpath.'

'O-kay,' I said slowly. 'So what you're saying is...'

Rounding the bench, I looked at the image from the other side. The picture was of a man being buried under a massive pile of money. Actually, it was a very *ugly* man being buried, a chubby man with a bad combover. There was no mistaking the resemblance between him and a certain local businessman.

'Uh,' I said. 'Aren't you concerned that he'll see this?'

Irene Everson answered. 'He will see it,' she said. 'Eventually. But this side faces the road, and you only notice it if you're walking on the other side. Giuseppe Costa rarely walks anywhere. He might not notice for days.'

'Maybe even weeks,' Nan added, grinning.

I shook my head. 'You women really *are* terrorists.'

'Never mess with yarn bombers,' Thelma said soberly. 'We're tougher than we look.'

'Well,' I replied, 'you look plenty tough to me. I'm glad we're on the same side.'

I continued back home with Trixie, where I picked up my car and headed over to Kim's place. She lived in a small brick cottage in Cape Carson, a few streets back from the Great Coastal Road. Her front yard was one of the most overgrown in town. An enormous bougainvillea dominated one side with an orange jessamine on the other.

I tooted my horn, and she trotted out.

'Have you ever thought about getting a gardener?' I asked.

'After what happened to Celia? Are you kidding?'

She climbed in, gave Trixie a quick pat, and we took off. A few minutes later, we were pulling in through the front gates of Sandcastle Village. We'd been here so often that it almost felt like a second home. Stopping in Doris's driveway, I turned off the engine, and we listened to the silence.

Well, almost silence. There was one pervasive and repetitive sound.

'Goodness,' Kim said. 'It's Princess—again.'

'How horrible. Can you imagine living with that day and night?'

We walked around the circuit to Hannah's home, as the endless barking continued. Trixie gave an answering reply. There was something in the sound that made me pause.

'Hey girl,' I said. 'What is it?'

Hannah's car was nowhere to be seen; presumably, it was in her garage. We made our way up to her front door. I was about to knock when it creaked open slightly.

'Hannah?' I called. When there was no answer, I turned to Kim. 'What do you think?'

She rolled her eyes. 'Come on,' she said. 'Hannah may have

had a medical episode—for real.'

Pushing open the door, Princess' barking grew even more frenzied, and then the little pug came charging down the hall. Instead of stopping, it tore past us and out the front door. Kim and I silently exchanged glances before continuing down to the kitchen.

'Oh dear,' I said.

Hannah lay dead on the kitchen floor, a kitchen knife jammed into her chest. A small patch of blood soaked her dress. I quickly checked her pulse, but she'd been dead for some time.

'That's an identical method as Felix Kent,' Kim said.

'Hannah's wearing the same dress as last night. She must have been murdered soon after I saw her.'

'But why kill her?'

An idea was already forming in my mind.

'Last night Hannah talked about going on a holiday,' I said. 'That means she had money. Or would have it. I bet she was trying to blackmail the killer.' I nodded to her body. 'It didn't go well.'

'Wait a minute,' Kim said. 'What's that smell?'

I inhaled deeply. Kim was right. There was a scent in the air. Something I recognised. Crossing to the kitchen tidy, I pushed on the pedal, and it flipped up.

'Pizza wrapping,' I said. 'From Penny's Pizza Place.'

Kim peered into the bin. 'There's a lot of wrappers in here,' she said. 'Hannah must have been a regular.'

'Maybe that's how she knew Felix Kent.'

'Good grief.' Kim looked closer. 'It's ham and pineapple. Hannah and I would *never* have been friends.'

I stared into the bin. 'You know,' I said. 'Those wrappings are fresh. Hannah and her killer may have shared pizza.'

'So we're after someone who likes pineapple on pizzas.' She shook her head. 'There are some strange people in this world.'

I reminded her that there were many nice people who loved pineapple on pizzas who didn't commit murders. Then I rang Todd and gave him the news about Hannah. Soon half a dozen police were swarming over the site. Todd asked us what we knew and then told us to stay close by. As Doris had given me a key, we went to wait in her home.

I rang her with the news.

'Good Heavens,' she said. 'Hannah's dead? And you think she was trying to blackmail Celia's killer?'

'That's our theory.' I explained that the police were searching Hannah's place for clues. 'They may find something worthwhile.'

'Thanks for letting me know. Hang on. Harry wants to talk to you.'

She put me through to his phone, and he asked me how the investigation was proceeding. I brought him up to date on everything.

'Frankly,' I said. 'I'm feeling a bit lost. Everyone hated Joe Porter and would have been happy to see him dead. We've got plenty of suspects and no smoking gun.'

'Maybe I can help,' Harry said. 'You know I was a journalist for thirty years. You're not the only one who can write stories. I have a few favours I can call on. People I know who may be able to help.'

I thanked him and hung up. There didn't seem to be a lot to do then. We sat in Doris's home, watching the police go in and out of Hannah's place. A forensic team arrived and removed items from the home. Two hours passed before Todd knocked at our door and came in to speak. We sat down in the kitchen.

'It seems I owe you an apology,' he said.

'Huh?' I said.

I'd expected him to yell at us.

'You found something?' Kim guessed.

'We found plenty. There was a roll of money in a jar in Hannah's kitchen. A thousand dollars. That's a lot of cash to keep at home.'

'That was the payoff,' I said. 'She was blackmailing some-one—or trying to.'

'We've dusted for fingerprints, although I'm not holding my breath. It looks like the killer wore gloves.'

Kim asked, 'What was the time of death?'

'Sometime around ten o'clock. No later than midnight.'

'And you're interviewing all the residents?' I asked.

'We are.' Todd looked pained. 'Can you stay clear? Is that possible?'

As much as I wished I could accommodate this, I couldn't. 'Todd,' I said. 'I've got a job to do. The same as you.'

'Then just stay out of my way,' he said. 'Please.'

Without saying another word, he left the room. I'd never seen Todd look so unhappy. I felt as if I'd done something terrible to him, but I didn't know what. 'What was all that about?' I asked.

'Rosie,' Kim said. 'He's *disappointed*. We told him about Celia and Joe, and he didn't listen. Now Felix and Hannah are also dead.'

Kim was right. We'd warned Todd, and he hadn't listened. I'd be disappointed, too, except it wasn't strictly his fault. *No*, I thought. *It's not his fault at all.* The person responsible for this was the killer. They were the one who had wrought all this destruction.

'Then there's only one way to make this right,' I said. 'We've got to catch the killer.'

22

'Naya?' I said. 'Do you mind if we speak to you?'

We were standing on the doorstep of the psychotherapist's home. 'Mind?' she said, peering past us. 'Are you kidding? I need to know what's happening! What's going on at Hannah's place?'

The police had obviously not spoken to her yet. I explained about finding the woman dead.

Naya's mouth dropped in amazement. 'What?' she said. 'That's horrible.'

'I'm sure the police will talk to you shortly,' I said. 'May we come in?'

She allowed us inside. Ramona was in the kitchen, pouring coffee from a pot. Naya offered us a cup, but we declined.

'Can I ask you where you were last night?' I began.

Naya cast a sideways glance at Ramona. 'Why do you want to know?'

'Because the police will want to know.'

The woman's gaze met ours. 'I was home all night,' she said. 'I had counselling sessions with several clients.'

Kim spoke up. 'And when did they finish?'

'Around ten o'clock.'

'And after that?'

Naya's jaw tightened. 'I went to bed,' she said. 'Ramona can vouch for me.'

Our eyes crossed to the personal assistant, who nodded. 'Yes,' she said. 'Naya was here all night.'

I didn't know what to say. It was as if the air had been pressurised. The tension had increased tenfold—and there was nothing I could do about it. I couldn't challenge them. That would be a mistake.

'Just one last question,' Kim broke in. 'It's about...pizza.'

Naya's face fell. 'Pizza?'

'We're doing a survey. Are you much of a fan?'

'I suppose everyone likes pizza.'

'Ham and pineapple?'

Naya forced a smile. 'Those two items should never share a pizza together.'

I nodded thoughtfully. Naya could be lying. It was hard to say. 'Thanks,' I said. 'We'll be in touch.'

Naya saw us to the door. 'Do the police have any leads?'

'They have some ideas. It's still early days.'

Soon, Kim, Trixie, and I were back on the footpath just as

the gates to the estate wheezed open. Doris drove through, and we followed to her driveway, where she got out of the car. 'So we've got another death,' she said, grimly. 'Which probably makes me a suspect too.'

'Everyone's a suspect,' I told her. 'I'm even looking at Kim funny.'

'Hey!' Kim protested.

'Fortunately,' Doris said, 'I have a cover story, although I almost wish I didn't. Violet suffered a bit of a turn on Percy Street yesterday. She was taken to the hospital, and I was there till about midnight.'

'Goodness,' I said. 'Is she all right?'

Doris hesitated. 'Yes, but this week has been terribly trying for her. Leon's been in contact several times about selling the house. What with losing Celia, Violet's been quite stressed.'

'I'm sorry to hear that.'

I told Doris we'd speak again later. From the corner of my eye, I'd spotted Vincent Orr on his front doorstep, with his son Graham huddled behind him.

They were watching the proceedings. Kim and I hustled over. On our approach, Graham disappeared into the gloom of the house.

'What's happening?' he asked. 'Has there been an accident?'

'A murder, actually,' Kim answered.

'What?'

'Hannah's dead,' I told him. 'The police are interviewing everyone on the estate.'

Vincent's mouth fell open in astonishment. 'Well, that's terrible,' he said. 'I'm completely shocked.'

Are you? I wondered. *Or are you just pretending?*

We followed him in. Kim cast her eyes across the antiques as I focused on Vincent. 'Were you home last night?' I asked.

'I was. The entire night. I was helping Graham with his English homework.'

'You didn't see anyone strange about?'

'Not at all. I was busy, though, pricing some cutlery that arrived as part of a deceased estate.'

Kim had stopped in front of the dining room table. 'Oh my goodness!' she exclaimed.

Vincent crossed to her. 'Oh yes,' he said, panicked. 'Please don't touch that. It's quite valuable.'

On the table lay a single uncreased sheet of paper in a clear plastic sleeve. My eyes glanced across the typewritten letter and finally at the signature on the bottom. 'Ernest,' I said, unsure what could cause such excitement.

Kim's eyes met mine. 'Ernest,' she said. '*Hemmingway.*'

'Wow!'

Before I could look more closely, Vincent snatched up the letter. 'I'm so sorry,' he said. 'I'm selling this on behalf of a private buyer, and they asked me not to share the details.' He placed it in the drawer of a tallboy. 'What happened to Hannah is terrible. Was there anything else?'

'No,' Kim said. 'But we are wondering what you think about...pizza.'

'Pizza?'

'Yes. Pizza.'

'Pizza?' He seemed to struggle with the word. 'Pizza?'

This could go on all day. 'Yes,' I cut in firmly. 'Pizza. There are hundreds of different varieties.'

'I know that,' Vincent said, annoyed. 'We eat pizza some-times. Actually, we had some last night.'

'Really?' Kim said. 'Where from?'

'Giovanni's. They do a good pizza.'

He'd get no argument from me.

'Is there anything else?' he asked.

'What flavour?' Kim persisted.

Vincent frowned. 'Four seasons.'

I thanked him, and he showed us to the front door. 'Is there any point in wondering about my pizza preferences?' he asked.

'A survey,' Kim said. 'We're curious as to what pizzas people eat.'

We left and made our way to the street. When we were out of ear range, I turned to Kim. 'Seriously?' I hissed. '*We're curious as to what pizzas people eat?*'

'It's hard to subtly bring it into the conversation!' Kim

snapped. 'How do you broach a subject like that? *Hey Vincent, Hannah's dead and—by the way—what's your favourite pizza? She probably ate it with her killer.*'

I didn't want to argue. Before I could continue, however, I noticed Henry and Olivia on their front lawn, surveying the scene at Hannah's place. 'Come on,' I said. 'Now's our chance.'

We charged down the street. Henry caught sight of us. For a moment, he looked like he wanted to run in the opposite direction but knew it would look bad. Instead, Henry forced a smile. 'Hello ladies,' he said. 'We've heard the tragic news about Hannah.'

'She was murdered,' I said. 'The police are checking everyone's whereabouts for last night.'

'Really?'

'Specifically between ten and midnight,' Kim added. 'Where were you?'

Henry looked flustered. 'You're not the police,' he said. 'We'll speak to them, and that's all.'

'We have nothing to hide.' It was Olivia who spoke. 'We were home last night. Watched a movie. Turned in early. We slept the sleep of those who have been avenged.'

She touched the angel broach on her cardigan.

Huh?

'Olivia,' I said. 'What do you mean?'

'Nothing!' Henry snapped and turned to his wife. 'Oliva, my dear. You must rest. You haven't been sleeping properly.'

Olivia smiled vacuously. 'I don't need to rest,' she said. 'I've rested long enough. Vengeance is carried out. Justice is done.'

Henry turned to us, his face pale with fear. 'Excuse me,' he said. 'Olivia hasn't been well. She's skipped her medication and hasn't eaten.'

'Talking about food,' Kim started, 'I assume you ate dinner last night?'

Henry frowned. 'Yes.'

'Pizza?'

'Risotto.' He reddened. 'We've been nothing but civil to you women. Now I will request—no, *demand*—that you stay away from us. All of this has been a terrible shock. Keep away. Do not approach us again.'

'Henry—' I started.

'I mean it! I will report you to the police for harassment if you come near us!'

Olivia was staring into space, smiling and nodding slightly to herself. It was scary to watch. Something was going on in her head, although I had no idea what. Henry took his wife's arm and led her back into their home. As they disappeared inside, Kim turned to me.

'Well,' she said. 'That went well.'

Went well—?

'Kim. They threatened to call the police on us. I think it's safe to say that we won't be on their Christmas card list.' I paused, thinking. 'Olivia's clearly disturbed. She could be the killer. What with all that talk about vengeance being carried out.'

Kim nodded. 'Olivia could have murdered Joe Porter,' she said. 'Celia saw it happen, and Henry paid Felix to kill her. Somehow, Hannah found out, tried blackmailing Henry, and he killed her.'

It was a working theory. A good one, too, although we had no evidence for any of it. Plus, we still had people to interview. We continued past Hannah's place to Luca's home. Luckily, both he and Trudi were talking on his front lawn.

'Lovely ladies!' Luca said grandly. 'What a tragic situation. Our dear friend, Hannah, has been viciously murdered—and we wonder who will be next!'

'Hopefully, no one,' I said. 'Kim and I are speaking to everyone on the estate about their movements last night.'

'Last night?' Luca said, swallowing. 'I was home. I did not go out.'

But I saw you! I thought. *That was you driving down Percy Street!*

'Really?' I said.

Kim persisted. 'You didn't go out...for a meal?'

'A meal?' Luca paled. 'No. I was here all evening.'

Although it was clear he was lying, there was no point in pushing him. That would only cause him to deny it even more.

'I was out,' Trudi said. 'I've been doing a pottery course in the evenings at TAFE.'

'We've been doing a survey,' Kim said unexpectedly. 'About pizza.'

Luca swallowed nervously. 'Pizza?'

'Should pineapple be put onto a pizza?'

'No...' Luca said. 'I mean...yes. It is a good topping. A nice topping for a pizza, although I do not eat it myself.'

'What do you think?' I asked Trudi.

The woman raised an eyebrow. 'I don't like pizza,' she said. 'And I'm allergic to pineapple. Now if you don't mind, I have to get moving.'

23

'So,' I said. 'People have some pretty strong opinions about pizza.'

Kim and I were sitting at home with Nan around the dining room table. All our questions about pizza had resulted in us deciding to get home-delivered pizza for dinner—none of it, ham and pineapple. The day had been long and laborious, and not just for us. I knew that Todd had been busy conducting interviews. I'd rung him, but, as per usual, he'd had little to share.

'For some strange reason,' I grumbled. 'Todd wanted to investigate this mystery himself!'

Nan stifled a grin. 'The nerve,' she said. 'Almost as if it's his job.'

'Nan,' Kim said. 'It *is* his job.'

'I'm being facetious,' Nan informed her. 'Todd has a lot on his plate. If you girls are right, four people are dead: Joe Porter, Celia Spalt, Felix Kent, and Hannah Foyle. That's a lot of responsibility.'

An idea had been brewing in my mind all afternoon. After interviewing the residents of Sandcastle Village, I'd gone to work to complete some stories and write up what I knew so far about the case. The police could track down witnesses to collaborate everyone's statements; I couldn't. Ramona backed up Naya's alibi. Vincent said he was with Graham. Olivia and Henry said they were at home. Luca had lied about going out, and Trudi had said she'd been at a pottery class.

At least I'd been able to check up on her through a friend I knew who worked at TAFE. Trudi *was* at the class, but it finished at nine, which gave her plenty of time to return home and kill Hannah.

'I suppose our number one suspect is Olivia,' Kim said.

I nodded. 'She's the obvious one. The poor woman is clearly not of sound mind. The problem is that we can't corroborate anything she or Henry said.'

'And we're not exactly their favourite people,' Kim told Nan. 'Henry said he'd have us arrested if we spoke to them again.'

'Rosie has that effect on people,' Nan said. 'So who does that leave?'

'Naya was lying when we questioned her,' I said. 'I'm sure of it. And Luca was *definitely* lying. He said he was home, yet I saw him driving down Percy Street. Why would he lie?'

Kim spoke up. 'Rosie,' she said. 'I think we need to put Vincent on our list too.'

'He seemed nervous,' I agreed. And he only has his son to corroborate his alibi. You know what I think we should do?'

'Torture our suspects with ham and pineapple pizza until they crack?'

'That may not work,' I said, smiling. 'These people may secretly *love* pineapple on their pizza. No, I think we need to do an old-fashioned stakeout.' I suggested we park outside Sandcastle Village. 'Then we tail them and see where they go.'

'That could lead to a whole lot of nothing,' Nan said.

'I know,' I agreed glumly. 'Such is the life of a reporter.'

Kim nodded. 'And her faithful sidekick.'

Trixie barked.

'And dog,' Nan added.

Half an hour later, Kim and I were in my jeep, nestled in the shadows outside the gates of Sandcastle Village. This part of town was quiet during the day; at night, it became a graveyard. Kim and I took turns watching the gate while the other read their phone. Stakeouts in the movies are always portrayed as boring. In real life, they're far worse. Sitting in your car in winter is a sure fire way to catch pneumonia. After two hours, I had a crick in my neck and a growing headache. I was ready to give up when the gates began to creak open.

'Hey,' I said. 'Someone's coming.'

A dark-coloured Toyota trundled out of the complex and started up the road.

'That's Vincent,' Kim said. 'Follow that man!'

There was nothing Kim loved more than an old-fashioned car chase. Sometimes I wondered if she were a Keystone Cop in a previous life. We trailed through town after Vincent. It was almost midnight now, and most of the homes were in darkness. We reached Percy Street. The main road was silent and still. The restaurants and cafes had all closed. Boats in the bay rose and fell with the gentle motion of the waves.

Vincent slowed and pulled into the beach car park.

'Quickly!' Kim hissed. 'Pull over!'

I stopped the jeep under the shadow of a leafy eucalypt. Leaving Trixie behind, we scooted down the street to where Vincent had just left his car. He went to the boot and took out a cardboard archive box.

'What's he doing?' I asked.

Kim didn't answer. We clung to the shadows as Vincent looked about furtively, and then followed as he made his way through the silent carpark. Just as he reached the hill leading up to Cut Rock Lookout, he arrowed across the road to a council rubbish bin and dropped the parcel inside. He then took out a newspaper from his jacket and scattered it over the box.

What on Earth—

'He's dumping rubbish,' I said.

'Yes,' Kim agreed grimly. 'But what kind of rubbish?'

Glancing about one last time, Vincent made his way back through the car park. I drew Kim to one side. 'Should we follow him?' I asked.

'I think we need to see what's in that bin.'

'Could it be drugs? Maybe he's dropping them off for someone else to collect?'

'Seems an odd place for a drug drop.'

Vincent drove off and disappeared up a side street into town. Kim and I waited a few minutes before leaving our hiding place. We scurried to the bin and carefully extracted the cardboard box. Kim peered inside.

'What on Earth?' she muttered.

'It's a typewriter,' I said.

'An old typewriter.' Kim shook her head in annoyance. 'A Royal Quiet De Luxe, to be exact. He's dumping rubbish.'

'Great,' I muttered. 'Illegally dumping rubbish carries a twenty dollar fine.'

'This could be used as a murder weapon.'

'So can a kitchen sink, but none of our victims were killed with one. No, he's just decided to dump it rather than put it out with his regular trash.'

'Well, I'm not leaving it here. It's old. I'll donate it to Trash and Treasure. Someone will buy it.'

We returned to the car. By now, I was yawning and ready for

bed. Kim suggested we take a last look at Sandcastle Village to see if anything was happening. We were back on Sundial Drive a few minutes later and parked in the shadows again. The cold had enveloped Cape Carson like a frosty blanket. Stakeouts, I decided, were definitely for the birds. Next time, I was bringing blankets, biscuits, and hot chocolate. Make a picnic out of it. That's how stakeouts were supposed to be.

But that was for next time. For now, I was ready to call it a night.

'That's enough for me,' I said. 'I've had it.'

'Wait!' Kim hissed. 'Someone's coming.'

The gates creaked open again.

This time, a late model Holden came creeping out into the street. Kim and I stared.

'Wait a minute,' I said. 'That's Henry.'

There was something somehow furtive about the way he was driving. Almost as if he was desperate to remain quiet.

Henry drove down the road, and I restarted my jeep, leaving the headlights off as we followed. My stomach growled uncomfortably. It was well after midnight, and there was no good reason for anyone to be out and about. Cape Carson was shut up as tight as a drum. We passed through darkened streets. Only a few times did we see homes where lights were on. Through one window, I spied the flickering of a television. On the porch of a lonely house, a man sat smoking and staring into the darkness.

We trailed several hundred metres behind Henry. If he saw us, he gave no indication. Henry drove down to Percy Street and turned left, and crept slowly along the road. It was like watching a repeat of what we'd witnessed only an hour before. This time though, unlike Vincent, Henry didn't turn into the car park. He continued up the hill for Cut Rock Lookout.

'What's he up to?' Kim whispered.

'I don't know.'

Trixie whimpered.

I knew how she felt.

There was something awfully unsettling about this whole scenario. *Something is wrong here.* Henry's car turned into the lookout's car park. I dared not go any further, so I pulled over to the side of the road.

'It's too risky to continue,' I told Kim. 'You and Trixie stay here. I'll follow Henry.'

Before Kim could protest, I scooted out of the car and raced up the road. Keeping to the shadows, I stopped at a bend under a leafy tree and listened hard. The ocean murmured far below the lookout, as the water came crashing into the crevice. I'd been here hundreds of times but never at this hour and in such circumstances.

Henry's car had stopped, and the headlights were out. The car engine ticked slowly in the cool night. At first, I thought he may have still been in his vehicle. I peered more closely. But—no, he was standing like a statue at the guard railing, watching the ocean.

He slowly made his way along the railing, his eyes on the water below. Then he stopped as the barrier made a sharp turn around the vast crack that split the rock. Henry stared down into the heaving maelstrom. There was something frightening in his expression. A look of...what? Hate? Fear? Desperation?

Gripping the upper railing tightly, Henry lifted a leg to the lower rung as if to climb over. I gasped—and the sound was like an explosion in the darkness. Henry stopped and stared into the gloom where I stood.

My heart thudded like a V8 engine.

I was terrified, and my fear was for us both. Henry was unstable, and his self-destructive tendencies could be turned on me.

He can't see me, I thought. *It's too dark.*

Still, his eyes stared.

I dared not move.

We stayed like this as seconds turned into minutes. Then he abruptly turned and strode to his car. I didn't wait. As soon as he was inside, I sprinted back down the hill to my jeep. I climbed in just as he restarted his engine.

'Duck!' I gasped.

The three of us—Trixie included—sunk down low as his car

shot past us and down the hill. I remained motionless for a long moment before finally raising my head and spotting his vehicle, a tiny spot of light moving down Percy Street.

Kim leaned onto the dashboard. 'What was all that about?' she asked.

'I don't know,' I said. 'But something is terribly amiss in Henry and Olivia's household.'

24

We drove back through town to Sandcastle Village. It was after one in the morning, and we were all exhausted. Trixie was asleep on the back seat, lulled by the gentle movement of the car.

'Isn't it time we called it a night?' Kim asked.

I wanted to say *yes*. It had been a long day and an even longer night. I was tired, and my nerves were shattered.

Yet, somehow, I felt that this night wasn't quite finished. There was something else awaiting us. Deep down in my gut, I knew it. We stopped outside Sandcastle Village again. This time, Kim and I got out of the car and crept over to the gates. The estate lay in complete darkness except for a faint light emanating from a single household.

'Come on,' I said quietly. 'Let's take a look.'

We activated the gates. The sound of them opening was like a 747 in the quiet night. Kim and I scooted through and took refuge in the shadows. Nothing moved. We followed the road clockwise around the estate. At Henry and Olivia's place, their car was back in its driveway.

What was all that about? I wondered. *Was Henry about to jump into the water?*

And if so—why? Was it guilt for killing those people? Or was there another reason? Something involving Olivia?

We continued around the road until Kim grasped my arm. 'There,' she whispered, pointing. 'The light's on in Naya's house.'

We took refuge under a nearby tree where we could see a thin slice of Naya's living room. The chamber was lit by a solitary table lamp, its orange glow dowsing the room in a romantic light. Faint strains of music echoed out into the street. Something by Kenny G?

Goodness, I thought. *She needs to update her repertoire.*

Naya crossed the room with a wine glass in her hand.

'What are you doing?'

Kim and I bit back screams. The speaker's voice was low but devastatingly explosive as a figure emerged from the darkness behind us.

'Ramona?' I whispered, swallowing.

'You're not spying on Naya, are you?' she asked.

'What are you doing out here?' I asked, desperate to gain time.

'Insomnia,' Ramona said. 'I've had it all my life. I find that a late-night stroll helps me to relax.' She raised an eyebrow. 'It's amazing what you see. Owls. Possums. Voyeurs—'

Kim began. 'We were just—'

'It's okay,' the young woman said quietly. 'I didn't feel comfortable lying to you about Naya's whereabouts last night. It's positively stifling in that house. I can't take a step without Naya wondering what I'm up to.'

I stared at Ramona. 'Naya lied to us?'

She sighed. 'I shouldn't really say this,' she said, 'but Naya's not in there alone.'

My eyes shot back to the thin slice of the visible living room. At that instant, Naya came back into view again, and a man enveloped her in his arms.

'Good grief,' I said, stunned. 'That's—'

'Leon!' Kim said.

'They've been seeing each other for ages,' Ramona said. 'He even has his own remote for the gate, although Leon hardly ever uses it.' She paused. 'There's a break in the security system over Naya's back wall. Sometimes he scrambles across that.'

I tried to make sense of this. *Leon and Naya are dating.* Leon was a recipient of the will. What had Naya said about the day Celia died?

I had a doctor's appointment in town.

'The day Celia died—' I began.

'I heard you ask Naya about that,' Ramona said. 'I was

eavesdropping from the other room. Not one of my more ethical moments. Naya sent me out to do some chores that day. If she had a doctor's appointment, it certainly wasn't in her calendar.'

'Goodness.'

I needed to think about this. It was very late, and my brain was growing more addled by the moment. 'Can we speak some more?' I asked.

Ramona shook her head. 'I'm sorry, but—no. Please keep it to yourself, but I'm leaving soon. I can't stand the claustrophobic environment. It's not just Naya. It's Sandcastle Village. It's like living in a bubble.'

'You mentioned your mum being unwell.'

'Sorry, I made that up. I don't like lying, but I just need to get out of here.'

'At least you're dating a nice guy.'

Ramona smiled. 'He's asked me to marry him,' she said. 'It's all very sudden, and I still need to think about it. We're planning to drive up to Queensland. Maybe even do a trip all the way around the country.'

I nodded approvingly. That sounded like a great idea. Just the thing a young woman needed. Ramona said she was heading back in; there was a side door she used to avoid Naya. Wishing her a goodnight, Kim and I returned to my jeep. It was almost three in the morning, and I hadn't been up this late for years. I was about to start the engine when a vehicle came up the road and stopped outside the gates.

'Good grief,' I muttered. 'This place is busier than Southern Cross Station.'

'Do these people never sleep?' Kim murmured.

The car's passenger door opened, and the interior light came to life.

'That's Luca,' I whispered.

'And that's—'

25

'Mayor Lynch,' I told Doris Glow.

'*What?*'

I was leaning over the front desk at the Gazette's office. It was still early, and Doris and I were the only people in the office.

Doris leaned back in her chair. 'Mayor Regina Lynch,' she mused. 'And she's dating Luca Romero. Actually, that's not so surprising, now that I think about it. Although Luca is over the top, he can also be quite charming.'

Now wasn't the time for me to mention his bedroom, which looked like something from a seventies stag film. I'd been wrong about Jim Turner and Samantha Greco. Sometimes, the people who got into relationships were the ones you least expected.

'Have the police made any headway on Hannah's death?' Doris asked.

'Not that Todd has told me,' I said. 'I rang him, but he was *quite* uncooperative. It's almost as if he's trying to keep things from me.'

'He probably is,' Doris said wryly. 'I visited Violet at the hospital again last night. I asked if she knew Felix Kent, and she didn't.' She shook her head. 'The whole thing is like something from a Shakespearian play: the evildoer kills the assassin to tie up loose ends.'

The front door banged open, and Harry came lurching in. 'Good heavens!' he cried. 'Everyone's here before me.'

'Just us,' I told him.

'You got five minutes, Rosie?'

I nodded, following him into his office. Harry closed the door behind me, and I sat down as he settled behind his desk. It wasn't too often that Harry shut that door. It was usually something serious: a hiring or a firing. I didn't think it would be my firing, although times had been tough.

'No need to look so worried,' Harry began, producing a manila file from his overstuffed briefcase. 'I've been following up on your leads. First of all: Henry and Olivia Rudd.'

'That's right. Henry's the retired professor, and his wife, Olivia, was a bookkeeper.'

'She mentioned something to you about her son dying?'

'It was a hit and run,' I remembered.

Harry examined his notes. 'It happened about eighteen years back. They were living in Geelong at the time. The poor kid was on a pedestrian crossing when he was run over.'

Geelong was an hour south from Melbourne. 'They never caught the driver?' I asked.

'No. He was fleeing from an armed robbery. Got away with three hundred dollars from a convenience store.'

That's a small reward for taking a child's life, I thought.

'I found something on your antique dealer, too,' Harry continued. 'Vincent Orr was involved in an assault a few years back. Apparently, he sold something to an unhappy customer. A *very* unhappy customer. The man attacked him on the street, and the police were called. It never went to court, but there were lots of allegations.'

'Of what?'

'Fraud. The man who purchased the antique said it was a phony. A replica. Vincent Orr swore blind that the piece was real.'

Tom and Amanda had said Vincent had been in trouble for trying to sell cheap copies.

'What happened in the end?'

'Settled out of court.' Harry consulted his notes. 'I've got the lowdown on the other people in the estate too. This Trudi Kendrix was caught up in some kind of hacking scam involving digital currencies. Apparently, some passwords got stolen, and people lost a lot of money.'

I nodded. Trudi had mentioned her reputation being trashed online. This could have been part of that, or maybe she was involved in something illegal. I told Harry this.

'She could be innocent,' Harry agreed. 'It's impossible to say. Then there's Luca Romero. There's not much on him. Just a drink driving charge from about five years back. He was more than double the legal limit. He fell asleep at the wheel and ran into someone's car.' Harry studied his notes again. 'And, finally, there's this Naya Kapoor. You know she was sued by the family of one of her clients?'

'I heard something about it.'

'It was the wife of a Melbourne businessman. She suffered chronic depression and killed herself after getting some online counselling from Naya. Apparently Naya told her to drink green tea and meditate, and everything would be fine. As it turned out, it wasn't. Naya was sued by the family. Had to pay restitution. Her business closed down. Of course, all she did was set up again under a new business name with the same mumbo-jumbo and new marketing.'

I thought about Sandcastle Village. Everyone living there had secrets. Some very serious secrets. Although, I suppose everyone everywhere kept things to themselves. Things they never shared. Maybe Sandcastle Village wasn't different to any other place.

Harry was peering at me. 'A penny for your thoughts.'

'They're a jumble right now. This is like one of those classic murder mysteries where everyone did it.'

'Go for a walk. It always helps me.'

Harry gave me the file, and I put it away on my desk. Taking Trixie with me, I picked up a jumbo double-shot caramel latte from Sandy's and found an empty seat at the beach. Although the weather had been good the last few days, it looked like a change was coming. Huge clouds had gathered on the horizon and were heading our way. They'd probably hit us by nightfall.

Trixie chased a seagull along the beach. Shaking my head, I laughed. Dogs were great friends. They could pick up your spirits whenever you felt down. And maybe they taught us something about life, too; Trixie knew she would never catch one of those seagulls. The fun was in the chase.

'Wish I could do that.'

I turned to see Todd Parker crossing the grass with a coffee in hand. I must have only just missed him at the diner.

'I know what you mean,' I said as he sat down. 'One thing about Trixie. She takes the party with her.' I studied his face. 'You're looking very serious. Is it that black coffee? You know that stuff is undrinkable.'

He smiled. 'It's fine once you get used to it.'

'Yeah. Sounds too much like ham and pineapple pizza to me.'

'You don't like ham and pineapple pizza? Seriously? They're the best!'

I hit his arm. 'Are you mad?'

'Hey! That's assaulting a police officer!'

'And you deserve it, Todd! You're supposed to be setting an example to the community!'

Todd grinned. 'Rosie Ryan,' he said. 'You're the craziest woman I've ever met.'

'Good. I like to excel in everything I do. Now tell me why you're looking so serious. It's not like you.'

The big police officer shook his head. 'It's this case,' he said. 'The entire Cape Carson Police Department is working on it. There are even a couple of detectives flying down from Melbourne. I've rarely felt so hopeless. I should have listened to you when you first told me about Celia.'

Yes, I thought. *You should have listened to me.*

But I wasn't about to point that out. Todd needed a friend. Not a smarty-pants. Besides, as he always said, anyone could develop a theory. Cops needed evidence. Cold, hard evidence that pointed to someone as the killer. The case they took to trail had to be rock solid.

'Don't blame yourself,' I said. 'Both Joe Porter and Celia Spalt's deaths looked like accidents. It's only when the pressure was on that the killer panicked and stabbed Felix Kent.'

'And then Hannah Foyle. We found a burner phone.'

'Hannah was using it to communicate with the killer?'

'Yes. No names were used, probably in case everything went pear-shaped.'

'She was trying to blackmail the killer? How much?

'Fifty thousand.'

'Fifty grand?' I whistled. 'Did she say what she knew?'

Todd peered out at the water. Lightning flashed distantly on the horizon. 'No,' he said. 'I wish she had.'

'When were the first messages sent from Hannah to the burner phone?'

'Yesterday. Whoever sent those messages wanted to arrange a meeting at Hannah's home last night.'

'That's several days after Celia's death,' I said. 'Hannah told us she saw someone on the day Celia died who could have been a gardener. She didn't take much notice of them, but if she saw the same person talking to someone from the estate—'

'Then she put two and two together. Maybe she saw them at Penny's Pizza Place. That's where Felix worked. And we found wrappers in Hannah's bin.'

'Er, yes, we noticed those too.' I didn't want to admit that we'd done some investigating of our own before ringing him. 'She was a regular there.'

'There are no cameras at Penny's, and we've quizzed everyone who works there about Felix. They all say Felix was a loner. Apparently, he had a girlfriend, but we haven't been able to find her.' He mused. 'If Felix were my boyfriend, I wouldn't admit it either.'

I got up and walked to the edge of the path. Trixie had gone racing up to a young couple on the beach, and I called her back. The couple had their arms wrapped around each other. One produced a phone and snapped a selfie.

The woman was taller than the man. *Much* taller. It was a relationship that I couldn't imagine working—

And that's when everything froze. I stopped. I was staring at the couple and the beach, but I saw neither. Everything from the last few days had just come together.

'It makes sense,' I breathed.

Trixie, sensing my sudden change in mood, came dashing up to me as Todd stood.

'Rosie?' he said. 'Are you all right?'

'I'm fine.' My voice seemed to come from a great distance. 'But it's all just come to me. I'm pretty sure I know who did it and why.'

'*What?*'

I shook my head. 'Round up everyone. I need to speak to all the residents at Sandcastle Village.'

Todd rolled his eyes. ''Rosie,' he said. 'Can't you just tell me?'

'It's much less dramatic that way.'

'*Please?*'

'Okay,' I sighed. 'But can we get everyone together anyway? It's *so* much more fun.'

26

We were at the barbeque area in Sandcastle Village.

This seemed an appropriate place to meet. This was where it had all started. In this secluded spot, enclosed by curved benches, the barbeque in the middle, and the stepping stones leading across the pond.

The storm had come and gone during the night, leaving the ground damp. The benches were dry, though, and this is where everyone was seated. Everyone, that is, other than Todd and his faithful constable, Jim Turner. Another uniformed cop stood outside the circle, and I knew there were others patrolling the estate.

It was ironic, really. Sandcastle Village was built as a refuge away from the world. A place where people could feel safe.

Instead, it had become a trap.

Not every resident from the estate was here. Graham Orr was being cared for by a police constable. That was to spare him from what lay ahead. Violet wasn't there either. She was still in hospital, although her prognosis was positive. She would be out sometime in the next few days.

The other residents were here, though: Henry and Olivia Rudd, Trudi Kendrix, Vincent Orr, Luca Romero, Naya Kapoor, her assistant Ramona Coxon, and my co-worker, Doris Glow.

'When Kim and I first came to Sandcastle Village,' I began, 'we told you I was writing a lifestyle piece about the village and the residents. While it's true we wanted to know about all of you, it was for another reason. A new initiative, called the Storytelling Tent, was started recently by Kim, the head librarian of Cape Carson library. It allows residents to get up and share their memories of this area. The first session was quiet. There were only a few dozen people in the audience. But then someone got up who was going to change the whole atmosphere of the tent.'

'Must we sit through all this?' Vincent asked. He looked bored and annoyed. Of everyone in the estate, he'd been the one person who had practically refused to come to this meeting. 'I have things to do.'

'We're all busy people,' I said. 'But killers must be brought to justice.' I turned to bring my gaze to bear on each of them. 'And one of you is a killer.'

This announcement was met with dead silence. Henry Rudd swallowed hard and took his wife's hand. Her gaze met mine and then shifted to a nearby bush where a butterfly had settled. She watched as the insect took off and fluttered away into the undergrowth.

I continued. 'Celia Spalt stood up at the Storytelling Tent and said that she'd seen a murder. Of course, you all know what had happened to Celia. A stroke had affected her ability to communicate, and dementia was closing in on what remained of her mind.

'But on that day, she saw something that sparked a memory. And Celia did her best to communicate it to us. Of course, at the time, we dismissed it as an old woman's ramblings. Old people are like that, we thought. They're confused, and they don't know what they're saying.

'Except, we were wrong,' I said. 'Celia had seen a murder. She'd seen Joe Porter die.'

I cast my eyes over the group. Most of their expressions were unreadable, although a few were frowning. In Henry's face, I saw naked fear. He looked ready to run. By contrast, a smile played at the edges of Olivia's mouth as she played with the gold angel on her cardigan.

'A lot of people hated Joe Porter and they had good reason to. Joe Porter had won big on the lottery, and he wasn't afraid to let everyone know. But people hated Joe Porter for more than that. There was barely a person on the estate who hadn't argued with him.

'And Joe always took revenge. He wasn't the type to openly attack others. No, he operated behind the scenes. Hannah's dog barked continuously, and she found lumps of poisoned meat on her front lawn. Trudi complained about Joe leaving rubbish on the footpath and was slandered online. Olivia and Henry complained to Joe about being a Peeping Tom, and Joe responded by making their cat disappear.

'And it goes on. Luca's letterbox was stolen. Vincent's garden got ruined. Ramona, who works for Naya, had her car keyed. Everyone suffered at the hands of this terrible man. Everyone had a good reason to dislike him.' I paused. 'But did they have a good reason to kill him? That's the more important question. Luca's letterbox was stolen, but would he kill Joe? It doesn't seem likely.' I watched the group, moving my attention from one person to the next. 'You need a *really* good reason to murder someone.'

Trixie yowled, and I patted her head.

'Joe's murder was only the first,' I said. 'The next was Celia. Her bedroom was on the ground floor of her home. From here, she'd witnessed the murder and made the fatal error of announcing it at the Storytelling Tent.

'The killer, who happened to be in the tent, flew into a panic; Celia had to die. Whereas the first killing had been committed by—let's call them X—this time X persuaded a petty criminal named Felix Kent to murder Celia.

'Felix Kent worked as a cook at Penny's Pizza Place on Second Avenue. Felix killed Celia thinking that he would get a cut of the money. X, of course, never intended that to happen; the first rule of assassination is to kill the assassin.

'Felix was stabbed to death, and his house set alight with Kim and me inside.' I turned to her. 'It was only because of her acrobatic ability that we escaped alive.'

Kim nodded. 'Three years of gymnastics at high school,' she informed the group. 'Ranked third in the state for my age.'

'Then things got worse for X. You see, Hannah had seen X and Felix together, most likely near Penny's Pizza Place. And Hannah's game was blackmail. She wanted to bleed everything she could from X.

'Sadly, Hannah's blackmail attempts only led to her death. She underestimated the lengths that X would go to.' I stopped. 'That's four people dead—and again, we come back to motive. We know why Celia was killed. It was to cover up the death of Joe Porter. And we know why Felix and Hannah were killed.

'But what we don't understand is why Joe Porter was murdered. To kill him for the reasons I've detailed is—pardon the expression—overkill.'

'All right,' Vincent snapped. 'I've listened to this for long enough. Either tell us who killed Joe Porter, or I'm leaving.'

It was Todd who spoke. 'You're staying right where you are,' he said.

'You have no right to hold me here!' he snapped. 'I've done nothing wrong!'

'Liar!'

Everyone turned. Of course, the person who had spoken wasn't Todd or me. It was—

'Kim,' I said. 'Do you want to handle this part?'

'Sure,' Kim said, her mouth set in a grim line. 'I've always wanted to do this bit.' She stood up. 'Vincent, as you know, is a dealer in antiques, though a few people over the years have queried his ethics. There have been complaints—'

Vincent started again. 'I don't have to listen—'

'Rosie and I visited Vincent's home,' Kim cut him off. 'It's full of rare pieces. You can imagine how excited I was to see a letter by Ernest Hemmingway sitting on a table. Librarians love that kind of thing: old books, letters, and manuscripts. Anyone who loves books loves the way they're put together and the people who write them.' She clenched her jaw. 'Last night, Rosie and I followed Vincent and saw him tossing an old typewriter in a public bin. What made it even more disturbing was that the typewriter was in good condition.

'I couldn't just allow it to go into general rubbish. I decided to save the typewriter, so I took it to work and sat it on a shelf in my office. I kept glancing up at it. How strange, I thought, to throw something like that away. Why not donate it to Trash and Treasure? And why toss it into a public bin? Why not take it to your local recycling centre?

'And then I thought about the Hemmingway letter. I could see it clearly in my mind's eye. That old piece of paper with Hemmingway's signature on it. What a rare find. An honour to see such a thing in person.'

Kim began to pace. 'I kept thinking of the paper it was written on,' she said. 'I don't know why. The subconscious mind is a strange thing. It keeps working away, nagging at us, even when we're doing other things.' She paused. 'And I thought again about the Hemmingway letter, that beautiful *uncreased* letter.'

The word hung in mid-air.

'Why would a letter from Hemmingway be *uncreased*? It's possible, but most letters are *folded* for mail delivery. And then I remembered a method of fraud that forgers have employed. They cut blank pieces of paper—the flyleaves—from the front and back of old books and use these to write or type on. If experts examine the letter, they find the paper to be genuinely old. What's more challenging and more expensive is determining the age of the ink. Experts have to employ the dual process of gas chromatography and mass spectrometry to spot a forgery. Of course, we don't have that kind of equipment hanging around our library. However, I was able to examine the books in our own collection. People don't realise that when we catalogue books, we describe the front matter, flyleaves and end matter. We describe a book as both a written and a *physical* object.'

Kim tightened her fists, and her face grew red. I was genuinely concerned that she might physically attack Vincent Orr.

'You can imagine my anger—no—*rage* when I realised that someone had removed several of the flyleaves.' Kim turned to Vincent. 'That was you, wasn't it, Vincent? And that's why you threw away the typewriter. You panicked when Rosie and I saw the 'Hemmingway' letter. You were terrified that we'd realise what you were doing and the police would show up at your home. And that's why the letter was unfolded. It's never been mailed to anyone because *it's a fake*!'

Vincent looked ill. 'I...you have no evidence...'

'Those old typewriter ribbons are so helpful,' Kim said, charging on like a steam train. 'Everything you type leaves an impression on the ribbon. The ribbon in that typewriter has been used before, but the words are still legible.' She stopped. 'You're going to jail, Vincent, for a very long time.'

Doris spoke up. 'So did Vincent also kill Joe Porter and the others?'

'No,' I said as Kim resumed her seat. Vincent stayed on the bench, staring at the ground, unable to meet anyone's gaze. 'Someone else here is the person known as X, and that person is—'

27

'Stop!' Henry leaped to his feet, his face twisting with anguish. 'I confess! I killed Joe Porter! I don't know anything about the others, but I did it.'

This announcement was met with a shocked silence that was only broken when I spoke. 'Henry,' I said. 'Please sit. I know what you're trying to do, and it's unnecessary.'

'But I...I'm the one who killed him...'

'No. You didn't.'

During this exchange, his wife had been watching him. 'Henry,' she admonished. 'The woman's telling you to sit down. Maybe she knows about the angels too.'

'My dear.' Henry fought back tears. '*Please.*'

He slumped onto the bench beside Olivia, where she took his hand. 'Angels are all around us,' she said. 'They act on behalf of a higher power.'

'What are you saying?' Trudi demanded. 'That Olivia killed Joe Porter? And Celia? And—'

'No,' I said. 'Joe Porter treated everyone here badly, but none so badly as he treated Henry and Olivia. They had an argument about Joe's Peeping Tom activities, resulting in a fistfight between the two men.' I paused. 'Of course, there was another argument. Trudi and Joe argued about rubbish on the footpath. Henry and Olivia intervened and calmed everyone down. It was Olivia who very kindly disposed of the box of trash that Joe had dumped.

'I expect she was like most of us. Olivia took the box inside, probably glancing at the contents. Nothing in there would have been too interesting. After all, it was junk. That's all. Just junk.'

Henry's eyes filled with anguish. 'It was junk,' he muttered. 'But among the junk...'

'Among the junk were license plates,' I said. 'People sometimes keep old license registration plates as souvenirs. But these weren't souvenirs. These license plates had been stolen and put on a getaway car used in a robbery. That car struck and killed Olivia and Henry's son. The vehicle was never found, and the driver never caught.

'The number on those stolen plates would have forever been emblazoned on Henry and Olivia's memories. How could you ever forget it? The vehicle that killed your only son as he crossed the road? And, suddenly, here was the plate in Olivia's hands. And it all came together in her mind. Joe Porter was the man driving that day. *He* was the man who committed the armed robbery and ran down their son.'

I swallowed. 'Would I want to kill such a man?' I asked.

'You bet. Most of us would. A man hits a child at a pedestrian crossing and drives off. You can imagine Olivia's anguish. And how it tied in with her own beliefs about angels. Those angels had finally delivered the killer to them. It was time for revenge. Retribution. Justice. You can imagine her seeing Joe in the park and snatching up the stone to bring down on his head—'

'Please!' Henry screamed as he leaped to his feet again. 'No! It was me! Me!'

'Henry,' I said. 'It wasn't you—and it wasn't Olivia either.'

'What?'

'I can understand how you'd feel, thinking your wife had killed Joe Porter. But she didn't do it, Henry.' As he fell back onto the bench, I remembered Henry at Cut Rock Lookout. How, filled with despair, he'd watched the sea, wanting to end it all. Anyone would feel desperate and confused, thinking that their wife had murdered someone. 'People are killed for many reasons. Revenge is one of them, but the motive behind Joe Porter's death was quite different.'

This time it was Naya who spoke up. 'So the motive was?'

'One of the oldest reasons of all: financial gain.'

Doris frowned. 'But the inheritance goes to his niece,' she said. 'She lives in Marble Bar, out the back of nowhere.'

'The money does go to his niece, but she's not in Marble Bar. She's been among us the whole time.' I turned to Ramona Coxon. 'Haven't you, Kelly?'

The girl's mouth dropped. 'Kelly?' she stammered. 'That's ridiculous. I don't know what you—'

'Your name isn't Ramona Coxon. You're Kelly Porter. You're good. I'll give you that. Your Kelly Porter social media profile uses someone else's picture. All the images are from outback Western Australia. To a casual observer, it looks like Kelly Porter has made a life in one of the most remote locations in the country.

'You've been in charge of all of Naya's promotional material. Constructing a bogus social media profile would have been child's play.

'But you made a few mistakes. You said you came from Melbourne. Mordialloc, to be precise. The other day, I said it was lovely living near the water, and you replied, *I love the sea.* I thought it was a slip of the tongue or a misunderstanding. Mordialloc is on Port Phillip Bay; no local calls it the sea.'

'And what else?' Ramona demanded.

'That photo of you and your so-called boyfriend. He's probably a model that you've photoshopped into an image, which is why I thought he looked familiar. Supposedly, the photo was taken last month.'

'And?'

'The tree in the background is a jacaranda. That only blooms in spring and summer. This is winter. That means the photo would be at least five months old. Probably longer. There's no way that photo was taken last month.'

Hatred blazed in the woman's eyes.

'And?'

The single word was virtually spat at me.

'You insinuated that Joe Porter keyed your car,' I said. 'But that doesn't really make sense. You're driving an old Ford. Parked right beside you was Naya's car: a late model BMW. Why would Joe damage your car and not Naya's? She was the one with whom he had a grudge. You thought you were being clever by making yourself look like a victim. Instead, you drew attention to how odd it was that Naya's vehicle hadn't been damaged.

'And, finally, there was your hair. Naya mentioned you'd just had it cut. It wasn't a big deal. People get their hair cut all the time. But you cut it after you murdered Celia. You were worried that someone from the Storytelling Tent might recognise you. So you changed your appearance. I imagine you were sitting at the back—'

Then Kelly was on her feet screaming. She ran at me, fists flying, but Todd was too fast for her. He and Jim Turner wrestled her to the ground and slapped cuffs on the raging woman. They dragged Kelly to her feet. Her face was covered in dirt, spittle, and sweat, and her eyes blazed with hatred. All the while, Kelly Porter continued to snarl, saying she would kill me.

I didn't care. I was thinking of all the people who had died, but most of all, I was thinking of an old woman named Celia Spalt.

If not for her, Kelly Porter would have gotten away with murder.

28

The rain had set in.

It was coming down in huge sweeping gusts across the bay and lashing the front windows of Sandy's Diner. Percy Street was quiet. The diner was quiet too, apart from one booth. In that, five of us were huddled: Todd, Kim, Doris, Nan, and me. Trixie was settled out the front under the awning. I don't think the rain worried her one bit. Despite the wind and the storm, she was taking a nap.

'You know,' I said, 'Celia was really the one who brought Kelly Porter to justice. She had a habit of collecting things. *Stealing,* you might say. You remember Celia always wore that apron? And she was always tucking things away into it?'

'Aprons are handy,' Nan said. 'Though you can leave things in them by accident.'

'The day of the market, Celia stole a container of honey. Todd, you were there looking for the thief.'

'True.' Todd nodded thoughtfully. 'We didn't try too hard,

though. After all, Rosie, pilfering from a market stall is hardly a capitol offence.'

'Celia didn't know it was stealing. Her mind was too far gone for that. Later, she'd find whatever items she'd stowed in her apron and hide them at home. That's what happened the day Kelly murdered Joe Porter. After Kelly hit him over the head, she panicked and dropped the rock and ran.

'When I realised that Ramona Coxon was really Kelly Porter, I remembered one of the chests of drawers in Celia's house. Among other things, it contained a jar of honey and a rock: a red and brown rock. It's Joe Porter's blood on that rock. What she didn't reckon on was Celia seeing the murder from her bedroom window. Violet was out, so Celia went racing out to try to do something. By the time she reached Joe Porter, he was already dead. Celia saw the rock, picked it up, and returned home. By the time Violet returned, Celia had forgotten the whole incident and stowed the rock away.'

'I'm still trying to put all this together,' Nan confessed. 'My old brain doesn't work as well as it once did.'

'Your brain is working fine,' I assured her. 'Kelly wanted the inheritance, but she didn't want to wait. She removed all references to herself from the internet and created an entirely new profile. The pictures she used are from a complete stranger. The profile Kelly created made it look like she was living in the Australian outback. That last part, at least, was partially true.

Kelly did spend time in Marble Bar. She moved to Melbourne and used her graphic design skills to falsify her documents to get a job working for Naya.'

Doris frowned. 'But wasn't she worried that the police would look more closely at her?' she asked. 'After Joe's death?'

'Not at first. Remember, this whole scheme depended on Joe's death looking like an accident. Her deception wouldn't have survived intense scrutiny by lawyers and police. You can't just walk away with a six million dollar inheritance because you have a Facebook profile.

'But no one was looking at Joe's death. Everyone thought it was an accident. All Kelly had to do was wait around a little longer and then leave the area. She'd claim the estate, sell it from some remote location and start a new life.

'But Celia remembered the murder at the Storytelling Tent,' Kim said.

I nodded. 'Kelly was sitting in the back of the audience,' I said. 'Once Celia blurted out about the killing, Kelly knew she had to act quickly. Celia had to die. Kelly had already murdered one person and couldn't risk being seen going to Celia's home. That's why she convinced Felix to commit the murder. She'd been dating him for a while in case she needed someone to do some dirty work. As it turned out, she did. Kelly likely promised him money and a life together. He didn't know the depths of her greed. She never intended to let him live.'

Todd picked up the story. 'Kelly murdered Felix at his home,' he said. 'And then set fire to the building, also hoping to kill Kim and Rosie. Fortunately, they escaped, but Kelly's problems weren't over. Hannah Foyle was a regular at Penny's Pizza Place. Despite Kelly trying to keep her relationship with Felix secret, Hannah had spotted them together. She guessed what was happening and tried to blackmail Kelly.'

'*Tried* being the operative word,' I said. 'Kelly murdered her too.'

Doris shook her head. 'With all these deaths,' she said, 'I've decided to move out of Sandcastle Village. For a quiet place, it's way too eventful. I'm going to find a nice little cottage near the ocean.'

'Sounds good to me,' Nan said.

Kim was staring into space. 'It was both fortunate and tragic that Celia remembered the murder,' she said. 'It led to her death, but also to Kelly's arrest. If not for Celia, Kelly would have gotten away with Joe's murder.' Her brow furrowed. 'I wonder what triggered her memory.'

I smiled. 'I think I know what Celia saw,' I said, turning. 'She saw *you*.'

'*Me?*' Kim squeaked.

All eyes swivelled to Kim.

'You remember the t-shirt you wore on market day?' I asked.

'Yes,' Kim said, thinking. 'You mean...'

'It has the photo of the writer Truman Capote on the front and a quote. Of course, Truman Capote was the author of the story *Breakfast at Tiffany's*. That's probably what triggered Celia's memory. Kelly looks remarkably like a young Audrey Hepburn, who starred in the film. Celia saw the author's name, remembered the film and Audrey Hepburn, and made the connection to Kelly Porter. It all came back to her. She remembered the murder and tried to tell people, but no one was listening.'

Not even me, I thought ruefully.

'Goes to show that you can't dismiss old people,' Nan said. 'Just because we're old doesn't mean we're dead.' She nodded to the window. 'Looks like the rain's stopped.'

'Anyone feel like a walk on the beach?' Todd asked.

'Why not?' I said.

We headed down to the water's edge. Although the rain had stopped, the wind was still coming in hard. The others walked ahead while Todd and I strolled along behind.

'Thanks for having my back,' Todd said.

I looked at him with surprise. 'What do you mean?' I said. 'I've always got your back. You're one of the good guys.'

'Rosie Ryan,' Todd said, shaking his head. 'You're a special kind of woman.'

'I know. Just don't forget it.'

At that moment, the skies opened up again, and the rain came tumbling down.

Laughing, we scrambled for shelter under a nearby tree. Thunder rolled across the sky. What began as a shower became a deluge as we watched the rain. Todd smiled and put an arm around my shoulder.

I didn't mind one bit.

But the adventure doesn't end here!

Catch Rosie's next mystery in:

Aliens, Apples and Murder!

ABOUT THE AUTHOR

Darrell Pitt is a prolific author, with more than two dozen novels in print. Writing for both young and old alike, Darrell's books traverse multiple genres including cozy mysteries, science-fiction and adventure stories. A proud resident of Melbourne, Australia, Darrell shares his home with his wife and says he owns too many books (as if such a thing were possible!)

His literary journey began with a passion for crafting short stories in his youth, eventually evolving into full-length novels. Among his accolades, "A Toaster on Mars" earned a prestigious spot on the shortlist for the 2017 Russell Prize, showcasing Darrell's unique brand of humour. His novel, "The Firebird Mystery", received commendation from The Children's Book Council of Australia as a Notable book in 2015.

Darrell's Teen Superhero series has garnered widespread acclaim, while his Rosie Ryan books are a series of delightful mysteries set in a distinctly Australian environment. Among the books he's currently working on are a tech-thriller, a time-travel novel, and a mystery book set in 1960's Victoria.